DIRTY LITTLE SECRET

A Sweetwater Resort Novel

T. R. Hill

T. R. HILL

For my early readers—
I cannot thank you enough for your support and encouragement on
this journey. Enjoy your stay at Sweetwater Sun & Sport.

CONTENTS

PLAYLIST

❀ ❀ ❀

"Dirty Little Secret" by The All-American Rejects

"Feelin" by The La's

"Anything Could Happen" by Ellie Goulding

"One Week" by Barenaked Ladies

"A Little Less Sixteen Candles, A Little More 'Touch Me'" by Fall Out Boy

"Good Riddance (Time of Your Life)" by Green Day

"Your Love" by The Outfield

SWEETWATER SUN & SPORT RESORT GROUNDS MAP

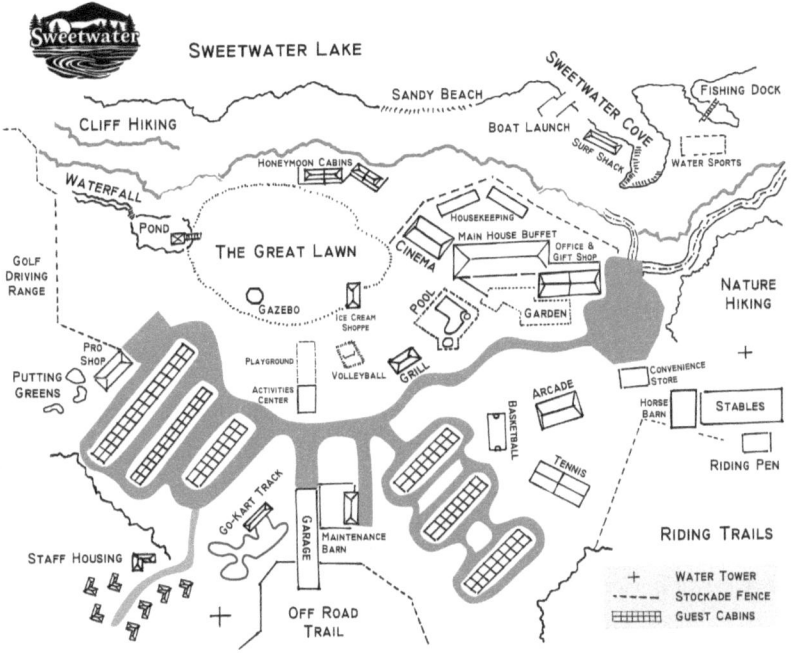

CELEBRATE, COMMISERATE, FORNICATE

Thursday, May 21, 2009: Kellyn

"Never have I ever hooked up with a guest," Kade says, challenging the rest of us heathens with a huge grin. The campfire glow settles on the faces of my coworkers and friends, and one by one, we all take a drink. All except Kade, my brother, of course—he's the last puritan in Sweetwater.

"One of these days, you're gonna slip up and join us on the other side," his best friend, Dane, says. "Hell, look—Teak's already crossed over." He razzes Teak's mop of dark curly hair, but Kade just laughs, shaking his head, halo still intact.

"I got one," Teak says, pride rolling across his baby face. "Never have I ever hooked up with a coworker."

Well, shit. There goes the group. To be fair, Teak's the youngest and newest staff member, so he's hardly had a chance to muddy the waters with his Sweetwater Sun and Sport coworkers—although he *is* Heidi's brother, and she's not one to waste time. Granted, her supermodel looks and perfect body hurry things along.

1

Quick glances and nervous laughter bounce among the remaining eight in our group, and Vinny's dark eyes find mine for an instant as flames dance in the space between us. It's a split second of contact but enough to burn. I finish off my drink and stand up, then walk over to the ice chest and pull out a bottle of water. I have a one-drink rule tonight and a week's worth of work to do tomorrow.

"Morning's gonna be rough," Merren says as she walks up beside me and grabs a bottle. My best friend and roommate, Merren McGrath, is a lightweight, but she's also the only one you want taking care of you when you're hungover. She could be a doctor or nurse with her bedside manner, but instead, she's here with me, working at my family's lake resort.

I nod and climb onto the tailgate of Kade's truck. Tomorrow marks the start of a new summer season, which means eleven weeks of serving resort guests with a smile, dodging whatever craziness they throw our way, busting our asses to keep things running smoothly, and sneaking down to the lake on Thursday nights to let off steam and salvage what's left of our sanity before the next round of chaos begins.

Merren joins me on the tailgate, pulling her light brown, stick-straight hair into a ponytail. "I can feel the hangover coming. Why do we do this to ourselves?" she asks with a half-laugh, half-groan.

"I don't know…to celebrate…commiserate–"

"Fornicate," JT adds, reaching into the ice chest and opting for another beer instead of water. He pops the top and chugs it, looking like a modern-day Greek god of Sigma Epsilon Xi.

"He's not wrong." I shrug.

When JT comes up for air, he crushes the can in one hand and drops it to the rocky lake shore as he stalks toward me like a lion hunting its prey. "Finally taking me up on my offer, Kell?" he asks, a devilish grin tugging at his lips, but I hold my hand out, keeping him at arm's length.

"Yeah, Kellyn." Merren nudges me. "How can you resist Sweetwater Sun and Sports' own Casanova?"

"I've managed this long," I say. "I think I can make it another season."

"Still hung up on someone else, huh?" JT asks, raising an eyebrow knowingly.

I give him a teasing shove and stand up. "Whatever you need to tell yourself to comfort that bruised ego, buddy."

Feigning hurt, he clutches his faded twentieth-anniversary resort tee shirt and stumbles toward Merren, making a show of it. Sure, he has the kind of jawline most girls fantasize about, and he knows how to work that panty-dropping smile of his, but I could never hook up with JT—he's too much like another brother to me. Plus, I'd rather not be counted as one among the millions. And with Jud Taylor, that's exactly what I'd be. The guy doesn't even have to lift a finger, and girls flock to him. Whether he does it intentionally or not, he's the biggest flirt I've ever met, and he's known for putting his talents to good use among the female staff—no, scratch that—the general female population in a twenty-mile radius, guests included.

Leaving Merren to comfort JT's "broken heart," I walk down to the shoreline and kick off my flip-flops, stepping into the cool lake water as the gentle breeze laps it against my ankles. It's quiet and peaceful out here tonight. Soon it will be buzzing with families and windsurfers, fishing gear and pontoon boats, wave runners and jet skis. And for three months, Sweetwater Lake will hardly see a break from the excitement.

"She's beautiful, huh?" Kade asks, coming up beside me. "Easy to see why Granny Kay insisted on building the resort here all those years ago."

I wrap my arms around myself as the breeze tickles goosebumps to life on my skin. There's something magical here, and it's no wonder my grandparents chose this spot to build their dreams. "Remember the story she used to tell us about the water spirits?"

"Of course," Kade says, making a face. "How could I forget?"

Granny Kay is a member of the Choctaw Nation and loves to share her tribe's legends and lore with us. As a kid, one of my favorites was the story of the water spirits.

"I remember coming down here with her during the off-season when I was maybe four or five," I say, looking out over the dark waters. "It must have been one of the first times I took notice of how different things are when summer ends—so quiet and empty." Kade nods and I chuckle at the memory. "I told her I didn't like being here without all the people. Then I made a big scene, pouting and complaining that it wasn't fun being here alone."

"You? Surely not," Kade says in his dry, funny-without-even-trying-to-be way. I kick my foot up to splash him with water for teasing me.

"That's when she told me about the creatures that live in the lake—how we're never alone here, even if it looks like we're the only ones around."

"The water spirits are always protecting the lake," Kade says, recalling the lore. I stare out at the onyx-like plane reflecting the slice of silver moonlight in the dark sky above, breathing in the fragrance of summer nights and wild freedom, the fragrance of Sweetwater.

"She said if ever need help, I can come to them for guidance and healing."

Kade squats down and runs his fingers in the lake, scooping cupfuls and letting the water run through his hands. "She told me that's why they call the lake Sweetwater."

"Fuck you, Dane!" Morgan yells, her voice breaking the silence and peace. I turn around and watch her stomp away from the campfire in a huff, ponytail swinging, as Dane walks toward the Surf Shack, head down and kicking rocks.

"You going to check on him?" I ask Kade, but he snorts out a laugh and stands up.

"They'll be over it before morning. It's like their foreplay."

"How sweet." I pick up my flip-flops, carrying them as my feet dry in the midnight air, and we make our way back to the fire pit, picking up any trash we find along the way. In the distance, I hear muffled wailing—

likely Morgan crying about Dane. They're worse than Ross and Rachel and borderline toxic. No one here expects them to get through the season without a nasty breakup, but we don't expect them to finally call it quits either.

I look around for Merren, wondering if she finally succumbed to JT's charms, but she's wrangling camper chairs and loading them into the back of Kade's truck.

"I'll kill the fire," Kade says, handing me the trash he gathered on our way back up shore. I toss it in the nearby trash can on my way to join Merren. We dump the ice water from the cooler and hoist it into the truck bed.

"Guess we know the party's over when Morgan and Dane start fighting," I say, shaking my head at the predictability of it all.

Merren rolls her eyes in agreement. "Like clockwork." With hands on her hips, she surveys the area as I shut the tailgate. "Is that everything?"

"Think so," I say.

Across the way, the fire dies out, and Dane ambles to the golf cart with Teak, JT, and Vinny following behind him. I slip my dry, dirty feet into my flip-flops as Kade walks by, and I notice his eyes focusing on something behind me while a smile curls up one side of his lips. I turn to see Merren on the receiving end of my brother's—what? Flirting? Desire? *Ew, god, no!*

C'mon, guys! I know it's just a smile, but it's the kind of smile that makes everyone around feel awkward. I love Merren, and I love my brother, but what the hell are they thinking? A match like that is the kind you want when you're ready to settle down and get married, not when you're in your twenties, working at a summer resort, and having fun. Merren's eyes jump from my brother to me, and she grimaces. She must read my face, which I have no control over—even when I don't say what I'm thinking, my face does it for me. And what it's saying now: *The actual hell, Merren?* Guess our rule to never fall for each other's siblings is out the window.

She opens the passenger door and climbs in as Kade walks around to the driver's side. Begrudgingly, I join them, knowing this ride will be awkward as fuck.

"Windows up or down?" Kade asks once we're all inside.

"Down," Merren answers before I have a chance. Fuck. I feel like a third wheel already.

Kade turns up the radio and Kenny Chesney's "Summertime" fills the cab. As we drive back up the hill to the main grounds, I refuse to look anywhere but out the passenger window. I'm not getting stuck in the middle of whatever *this* is. We come up on the boys in the golf cart, eliciting a ruckus of hoots and whistles as we do. Kade honks and flashes the headlights, and the next thing I know, Teak's white ass is on full display.

"Oh, my God, he's going to blind us."

"Looks like a full moon, baby!" Kade hollers out the window as we drive by, the whole lot of them screaming like wild banshees. Even Merren and I are laughing, and for a second, things are back to normal—feeling young and wild and free. It's the start of another crazy summer at

Sweetwater Sun and Sports Lake Resort, and I wouldn't have it any other way.

AND THAT'S WHY WE DON'T CATCH FEELINGS

Thursday, May 21, 2009: Vinny

The truck's tail lights fade like a comet as we climb the hill, the golf cart giving its all to lug our motley crew up the incline. Dane rides shotgun with a scowl, still worked up over Morgan's latest bitchfest, and behind us, Teak and JT laugh about tonight's mooning. I'm losing my buzz and thinking how the night could have ended differently—sneaking off with Kellyn and away from the others. Her salty, sun-kissed skin under my lips and the way her eyes blaze with something resembling a chaotic blend of madness and passion when she finally lets go.

Yeah, I'm thinking about it all right—with a little too much detail. I shift in the driver's seat and remind myself that tonight would never have gone that way. What happened last year was just a slip-up, a one—well, three-time—thing, and it's best we leave it that way, really. We're too different, and she's too fucking high-strung.

I shake the thought from my head and give the golf cart another push of gas once we reach the peak of the hill and the ground levels out. Now we're picking up speed, flying through the ghost town of Sweetwater Sun and Sport—one last night before it all comes back to life again. We roll past the main office and gift shop, perfect and pristine, awaiting tomorrow's rush. Then I notice a garden hose lying across the flowerbed wall and make a mental note to put it away first thing in the morning.

To our left is the arcade, followed by the basketball court, and a cluster of guest cabins. Only the globe lamp posts mark the darkness every hundred feet with their white balls of light resembling cotton crops. It becomes twice as dark as we travel farther into the resort, approaching the maintenance barn, golf cart garage, and employee housing. But this isn't a disservice to the staff or an oversight—we like it this way. When the guests arrive and take their carts out for a late-night spin, they avoid this area, opting for the main paths with better lighting.

I take a sharp turn to the left, and gravel crushes beneath the miniature wheels. "Your place or hers?" I ask Dane as we approach the first row of staff apartments.

"Not hers," he says, running his hands over his face. The best thing for Dane would be if Morgan took a job somewhere else and never came back. Those two are a walking disaster, but they never have been able to cut ties for good.

We roll past Morgan and Heidi's place, and I steal a quick glance at their neighbor's window. The lights are already turned off. *It's for the best. Don't think about her.*

Just up ahead on the other side of the path are two more units. I pull up and park the golf cart next to Kade's jacked-up Chevy. "You gonna be alright, man?" I ask Dane. He seems to be taking it harder tonight than usual. "Wanna come inside, blaze a joint?"

He drops his head back and blows out a long exhale before stepping out of the cart. "Nah, I'm just gonna hit the sack."

"Alright, see ya in the morning."

Dane slumps across the freshly cut grass to the apartment he shares with Kade, and I take the cart keys, shoving them in my pocket, before I make my way across the lawn. In front of me, JT ropes an arm around Teak, pulling him into a headlock. "And that's why we don't catch feelings, little one," he says, roughing up his hair before letting him go. Teak straightens up and then runs at JT's back, throwing himself into a tackle. I dodge their friendly row and head inside our three-bedroom unit.

The other two only moved back in a week ago, but trash spills out from the can, dishes fill the sink, and clothes lie scattered about the living room—some left by JT's conquests. It looks like a frat house, and I guess, in a way, that's what it is. We form a sort of brotherhood, working and living together all summer long. But some, like me, make it a year-long gig. While most of the college-age employees pack up and head back to school at the end of the season, I stay put, working maintenance with Mr. Cole, the groundskeeper. College has never been on my radar, and if it weren't for a falling out with my bandmates a few years back, I wouldn't even be working at Sweetwater.

I kick a purple bra out of my path and enter the hallway, passing two bedrooms and a bathroom before reaching a narrow flight of stairs that leads to my room, which is really more of a loft since it doesn't even have a door. At the top of the landing, I flip on the light switch, revealing a mess that's on-brand with the rest of the apartment. My queen-size mattress covers the floor, sheets all tangled up and clean laundry forming a mountain on one side. Across from that, a small TV sits on a plastic vintage milk crate, and my guitar—the only thing neatly put where it belongs—rests in its case against the wall.

I kick off my Chuck Taylors and undress down to my boxers and socks before stretching out on my bed. Beside me is a makeshift nightstand, which is putting lipstick on a pig—it's just the lamp and an alarm clock sitting on a large coffee table book of Fender guitar history. I set my alarm for the morning, and downstairs, I hear Teak and JT talking about the sort of girls they want to hook up with this summer. Teak's young and still getting his feet wet, so he's just after some action. JT, on the other hand, salivates like a dog waiting for fresh meat to hit the resort—he has to since he's already tried most of the options around here.

Rolling onto my side to get comfortable, I think about the campfire and her dark blue eyes catching mine for a split second across the flames. The glance we shared was too quick—the kind that tells others we're hiding something. I don't think anyone noticed it, though. Aside from JT, no one else knows what happened between us, and he only knows because he walked in on us—the second time.

I reach for my phone. The display illuminates when I push the button and start typing out a message. Then I stop, my thumb hovering over the keypad. It's almost midnight, and it's a bad idea—especially with the summer season starting tomorrow—she'll never go for it. I erase the message and toss my phone aside, then run my hands over my face and groan. *What the fuck is your problem, man? This isn't you.* I thought for sure nine months away from her would clear my head, or at least get her out of it, but the vivid memories of the three times we were together won't fade away, and I just can't shake her.

Kellyn Daniels is all business and rules and comes off as stuck up and aloof ninety-nine percent of the time, but I know what she's hiding. I know who she is in the dark, and it's intoxicating. But hell, I'm not looking for anything serious. That's the reason I agreed to her rules: *one time, no feelings, no one can know.* Except, one time became three. Maybe she was just logging practice hours before heading off to college—fine by me, happy to be of service—but now that she's back and stealing glances across the fire, I'm starving for another taste.

I get up and plod across the room to turn off the light. It's quiet downstairs now. Teak and JT must have finally gone to bed, and all I hear as I lie back down are the cicadas outside my window getting a head start on their mating ritual. The buzzing chorus isn't deafening yet, but it will only become louder between now and the dog days of summer—a cry into the night for a lover to share the season with. The poor bastards give it their all, singing to impress the ladies, and after a summer of love, they die off—but I guess they die happy.

As I chase sleep, the raspy cicada song takes me back to the first time I was with Kellyn. They were louder then—maybe they were lending me their song. Talk about wingmen. *Dammit.* Kellyn Daniels is the last thing I should be thinking about right now but the only thing I want to.

LIKE YOUR FACE?

Friday, May 22, 2009: Kellyn

It's nine-thirty and I'm already on my second cup of iced coffee. Good thing I followed my one-drink rule last night—today is not the day for battling a hangover. Even though the guests won't check in for a few hours, my morning to-do list is a mile long, and I don't want to miss a thing. Yes, it's my family's business and I take pride in its success, but it's more than that—I want to prove to my parents that I can step up and take on additional responsibility. I've been asking for a while, but they wanted me to graduate high school and get some college credits under my belt before talking about any kind of promotion, so I did. I just finished my freshman year with a 4.0 GPA despite working on campus twenty hours a week—thank you very much.

My parents already handed the water sports management over to Kade, and he's only four years older than me. Okay, so he's a certified windsurfing instructor and has his bachelor's in tourism management—but they let him take the reins years ago. Now, it's my turn.

I wipe away the condensation ring my iced coffee left on the front desk and triple-check that everything is stocked and ready for our first guests. We're fully booked for Memorial Day weekend, which is great, but it also means there's no room for slip-ups. With my clipboard in one hand and iced coffee numbing the other, I scan my list and walk around the front desk. The floor is swept, the plants are watered, and the complimentary mints are in the dish. Check, check, check.

Next, I step into the vestibule to inspect the activity display, straightening the calendar and information pinned to the corkboard. In addition to the daily activities planned for kids, teens, and adults, we're holding our annual summer kickoff party on the Great Lawn with local vendors, lawn games, and an outdoor screening of *Dirty Dancing* after sunset. My grandparents, who started the resort, fell in love with the film. It reminded them of their honeymoon in the Catskills, which they have always said was their inspiration for Sweetwater Sun and Sport.

Just behind the corkboard and to the right is the door that opens to a long hallway with floor-to-ceiling windows on one side as it winds around the building and ends at the main house dining hall. The hallway corrals the line of hungry guests at peak mealtimes, but it's also a hall of memories, a place where we display photos and keepsakes from years past, handwritten notes from beloved guests, and newspaper articles about our *home, Sweetwater home.*

I love walking through here, and so do our guests. It's like a 3D memory machine, taking you back to times you remember and some you only remember hearing about. From the vintage photographs of my grandparents breaking ground to the first staff polo, it's a special blend of nostalgia and promise. I breathe it in deeply before heading back out to finish my list.

✽ ✽ ✽

After an hour and a half of running all over the resort, checking with housekeeping to ensure all the rooms are ready, confirming the rental golf carts are fully charged and in working order, checking the sun deck loungers for breaks and tears, and a dozen other often overlooked details, I meet my parents as they're climbing out of their car in the main parking area.

"Here," I say, holding out the clipboard, confident they'll award me a promotion on the spot. "I've triple-checked everything—all the hiccups we faced on the last three opening days. See?" I point to my recently checked boxes.

"This is wonderful, sweetheart," my mom says, her sleek blonde bob falling over her sunglasses as she glances at the paper, shuts the Jeep door, and starts for the main entrance. "Thank you."

When my dad catches up to her, she hands him the clipboard. "Good job, Kell. Hardly a thing left for me to do." He winks at me and opens the door for us to walk through.

I follow them to the office behind the front desk area and wait for them to give me what I've been waiting for—what I've been working for. My mom sits down at her desk and goes to turn on the computer but realizes I've already done it. She starts clicking away, hyper-focused on her work already. Across the room, Dad pours himself a cup of coffee—the coffee *I* brewed before they got here. He smiles and hums a tune of appreciation after the first sip.

"So?" I ask, looking back and forth between the two of them.

"The coffee's great, Kellyn. Hey, Mel, you want a cup?" my dad says, turning back to the coffee bar.

"Sure, sweetheart. Is there any hazelnut creamer?"

"Yes," I say. "I made sure of it. So, can we talk about my role here?"

I might have come off a little abrasive. My mom stops her work and looks at me quizzically. "Kellyn, you know what your role is. It's the same as—"

"As every other year since I was fourteen." I groan and slump into the chair across from my mom's desk. "But I'm not a kid anymore. I'm almost twenty, and I went to college like you wanted—"

"You've only been one year, honey," Dad says, walking over and patting me on the shoulder.

"So? You guys let Kade manage the water sports before he finished college. What's the difference?" My frustration itches for a way out, and I start tapping my foot to release the energy. Kade always gets what *I* want, and it's not fair, but that childish argument won't help me today.

"What, exactly, do you have in mind, Kell?" my mom asks.

"I don't know…maybe activities director or guest services–" But I stop when I see my mom wince. Okay, managing guest services *would* be a tall ask, and maybe a little more than I could handle at first…but I'd rise to the occasion—I know I would.

"Activities director isn't off the table, but I'm not sure we're there just yet," Mom says, sliding her chair back and walking around to the front of the desk. "And with Merren doing so much in that area already… Well, I don't want to create an awkward situation for you two. You're such good friends, and you room together…" Mom crosses her arms. "No, that won't work."

I'm instantly deflated. Little does Mom know Merren might be on the verge of making things awkward between us anyway—but who knows if I really saw what I thought I did, and even if she and Kade are into each other and breaking our rule, it won't convince my mom to give me the job.

"Jake, do you have any suggestions?" Mom asks, and I turn to my dad, working my big blue eyes like the baby girl he knows I am. Hope springs back to life as I see a hint of a smile spread across his face.

"Well, you know… I just might have something, but I need to check a few things and talk to you about it, Mel," he says, turning his face to my mom. She nods and suggests that I give them some time to talk.

"Of course," I say with the most professional and level-headed voice I can manage. "Take all the time you need."

I grab my clipboard and head out to attend to my regular duties. I could do them in my sleep—I could do them blindfolded and one-handed. I could probably do them backward if I tried. They're the same mundane tasks I've been charged with for the last five years.

The sun heats up the asphalt as I make my rounds in the golf cart, and the familiar tar-sprinkled scent tells me summer season is here. I park in front of the activities center and head inside to make sure Merren has everything she needs for the weekend.

"Mer?" I holler as I open the door to the building and look around. "You in here?" The heavy door bangs shut behind me, and I step into the main room that's filled with tables and chairs. Sometimes it's a bingo hall, sometimes it's an arts and crafts room—sometimes it's damn near a daycare. It's whatever we need it to be to keep the guests happy and entertained.

"Mer?" I holler again, this time louder, as I approach the room marked "employees only." She should be here prepping for the guests, but it doesn't look like she's done a thing. Then the thought hits me—what if she's in there with Kade? I do *not* want to walk in on the most awkward and nightmare-inducing scene I can imagine. See, this is why we have rules, Mer—to save me from gouging my eyes out like Oedipus.

"Anyone here?" I ask, giving fair warning as I reach for the door, but it swings wide and Merren stumbles into me, balancing a stack of board games so high it covers her face. I manage to catch Trouble and Battleship, but Clue tumbles to the ground, spilling suspects and weapons all around us. "Oh, shit. Sorry." I bend down to help her clean up the mess.

"I didn't hear you come in," she says with a laugh, and I notice her bright red cheeks. It's not *that* hot yet, and this isn't *that* embarrassing… Plus, how could she not hear me? I was practically yelling. I know my best friend, and this is *not* normal. *Fuck my life.*

We stand up, and I follow her to the nearest table. "I didn't see game night on the weekend activities," I say, trying to recall the list posted on the bulletin board.

Merren brushes a few strands of sun-kissed brown hair out of her face. "Oh– No, it's not. I mean…" She shrugs. "I just thought I'd pull some out in case any kids come in asking for them."

"Sure…" I say slowly and notice how she avoids my eyes. She's acting super shady and I'm not a fan. "Anyway, I was just stopping by to make sure you have the supplies you need for the weekend. I can make a run into town if needed."

She looks around the room, hands on her hips, and hums as if she's trying to think. "Nope. We're set. Thanks, Kell."

"Alright, well…if something comes up, you know how to find me." I motion to the walkie-talkie clipped to my side.

"Yep," she says, followed with a tight-lipped smile—like she's waiting for me to leave. Like I interrupted her make-out session with my brother. God, I'm gonna puke. I head for the door, looking back over my shoulder before I step outside. As Merren divides the board games between two tables, a much-too-familiar smile creeps across her face. I know that smile—she's thinking about a guy.

I focus on my to-do list, hoping it will push all thoughts of my best friend and my brother—gag—out of my mind. The next stop is checking in with the grill to make sure everything is ready for our first round of guests —they always arrive hungry from their travels, and once that first rush starts, it hardly slows down until August. The grill is just up ahead, past the volleyball court.

When I walk inside, I see Morgan behind the register, counting change and making a note. She appears to be in a much better mood than the last time I saw her—maybe Kade was right and she and Dane already made up. She looks over and acknowledges me with a ruby-red smile that matches her shirt perfectly.

"Just making the rounds," I tell her. "Do you guys need anything here?"

Morgan pauses, then leans back and hollers toward the galley. "Where are we on buns?"

A few seconds later, Vinny walks up behind her, holding two commercial-size packages of hamburger buns. "We have these and two more."

"That might get us through tonight..." Morgan says doubtfully.

"No worries. I'll get more," I tell her and make a note on my clipboard before clearing my throat. "Can I speak with you, Vinny?" My tone is authoritarian and professional, and I catch Morgan making a face before she tells Vinny *good luck* and scurries away with the hamburger buns he brought out.

"What'd I do now?" he asks with a tone that tells me he's just biding his time and really couldn't care less what he did wrong.

"Your shirt, for one," I say, hugging the clipboard to my chest as I cross my arms. He looks down at his blue resort polo that's hanging haphazardly over the front of his waistband and catching on his belt. I watch him tuck the shirt into his jeans while the sun's heat sinks into my skin through the glass door behind me.

"Better, Boss?" he asks, walking toward me, his dark eyes set on mine.

"It's the wrong color," I say and take a step back, bumping into the table behind me. "Staff is wearing red today."

"Like your face?" he asks and hikes one corner of his mouth into a smirk, drawing my attention to the black lip ring there. I can feel his eyes watching me watch him as he flicks the piercing back and forth.

"It–it's on the schedule," I say, trying to compose my thoughts, which are almost entirely consumed by that damn lip ring and the way the cool metal feels on warm, delicate skin. *Fuck.*

Vinny steps closer, and his hand brushes my elbow discreetly. "You want me to take it off?" I close my eyes. He's too close. This is too risky. He smells too damn good. I grip my clipboard tighter and remember my mission: prove I can handle more responsibility. Fucking around with a Vinny is not part of that plan. For real this time.

23

When I open my eyes, I let out a quick huff and step out of his reach. "I want you to pay attention to the memos posted in the main office. They're there for a reason. Today is red, tomorrow is white, and Sunday is blue. It's not that hard to remember. And since you're…" I flip to the staff rotation schedule on my clipboard to confirm before I speak. "Since you're working the grill today and tomorrow, you need to take that out." I gesture to my mouth.

He pulls one of the dining chairs out from the table beside us, flips it around backward, and sits on it, casually draping his arms across the top of the backrest. "Still thinking about it, huh?"

"What? No– I don't know what you're talking about–"

"You keep staring at it."

"It's against policy when you're working in food service here."

"Mm-hmm," he says with a nod and a smirk that draws my eyes right back to the damn thing.

"Whatever," I shake my head and try to clear it from my mind. "If that's how you want to start the season, I'll just write you up and–" The glass door behind me opens, and I turn to find my mom.

"Oh, good. You're both here. I need to talk with you two," she says, leaving me utterly confused because she can't possibly be referring to me and Vinny as the *two*.

"Morning, Mrs. Daniels," Vinny says over the noise of the chair sliding on the tile.

"Let's talk in my office," she says and holds the door open for us to follow her. I feel like a kid going to see the principal. It's no surprise Vinny would be there—he doesn't care about rules and policies and uniform schedules—but *me?* I enforce the rules. I don't break them. Except maybe once…or three times last summer. And it wasn't a Sweetwater rule, it was one of my own. *Fuckin' Vinny.*

WE CAN'T STAND EACH OTHER

Friday, May 22, 2009: Vinny

Kellyn's freaking out. She's trying to act like she isn't, but she's wiggling her foot like crazy and tapping the armrest of the chair like a badass drummer. I don't know why she's so worked up—it's not like anyone knows about what happened between us, and even if they did, so what? We wouldn't be the first coworkers to fraternize over the summer. Unless her mom has a problem with *me*… But I don't see why she'd drag me in here to tell Kellyn she doesn't approve. It's not like we're together anyway.

"What's this about?" she asks her mom. Her tone has a sweet top note but doesn't hide the agitation at its core. Mrs. Daniels must notice it too because her eyebrows knit together when she looks across the desk at her daughter.

"Well, to follow up on our discussion this morning, Kellyn, I have a project for you and Vinny to tackle."

"Wait–what? Me *and Vinny?*"

Mrs. Daniels nods, and Kellyn turns to me like I have something to do with this. But I'm in the dark—I don't even know what conversation she's talking about.

"I'm sure you're both aware of the music festival we're hosting next month," Mrs. Daniels says. "We have most of the details nailed down, but we need someone to oversee the event—to make sure everything runs smoothly."

Kellyn sits forward excitedly. "I can do that. And, really, it sounds like a one-person job." She turns to face me. "You probably have a million other things–"

"You're working together on this, Kell," her mom says. "I have no doubt that you can organize the event, handle the PR–all of that, but you'll need Vinny's help with the execution and the grounds prep, the technical aspect...areas you don't have much experience in."

Kellyn slumps back against the chair somewhat dramatically, and it's hard not to laugh. "Thank you for the opportunity, Mrs. Daniels," I say, and as soon as I do, Kellyn gives me a look—it's a mix of annoyance and disgust, and before she looks away, I catch her eyes falling to my lip ring again. I run my tongue along the backside of it, pushing it out just a little, and watch as her cheeks turn red.

"You're welcome, Vinny. I'm sure you'll be a great help to Kellyn." She stands up and takes a file folder from her desk. "This has all the details and contact information. The permits and insurance are already handled, and the festival contact, Tyler–I think, is handling the tickets, advertising, and bands."

Kellyn and I stand up, and she hurries to reach for the file like she thinks I'm going for it, too. I'm not, but it's entertaining to watch her get all worked up. She always has to be in control, whether it's work or play, and she lives by her damn catalog of self-imposed rules. But I've seen her lose control a few times, and it was pretty fucking hot.

"Tyler will be here tomorrow afternoon around two," Mrs. Daniels says, handing Kellyn the folder. "He'll want to speak with you both, so either plan your lunch break around that time or find someone to cover for you."

I nod as Kellyn flips through the folder like she's looking for gold. Mrs. Daniels clears her throat and continues. "I expect you both to keep up with your regular work as well, so you'll have to find time to fit this in, but that's part of managing projects and business, isn't it?"

"Yes, ma'am," I say and smile. My words snap Kellyn from her focus, and I feel her laser-sharp blue eyes burning a hole in my profile. "If that's all, I better get back to work."

Mrs. Daniels nods and ushers us to the door. "Of course, thank you, Vinny."

As I walk through the main office and out the side door, I feel Kellyn sulking behind me, and I hear her huffs and puffs like a frustrated little wolf. But once I step outside into the heat, she strikes, grabbing my arm and turning me around to face her. "What the fuck, Vinny?"

"What?" I laugh and it just pisses her off even more.

"What's with the act? *Thank you, Mrs. Daniels. Yes, ma'am, I'm a little kiss-ass, Mrs. Daniels,*" she says with a much-too-whiny impression of me.

28

"You got a problem with me calling her Mrs. Daniels?"

"You know that's not what I'm talking about." She steps into my shadow and stares up at me, blue eyes blazing and blonde wisps of her ponytail flying free in the breeze. "Acting like you're employee of the month when you can't even follow the rules!"

"That's it, huh? *That's* what you're so worked up about? This?" I ask, untucking my shirt and watching her eyes as they follow my hands. "And this?" I flick my piercing.

Kellyn narrows her eyes on me and draws her lips tight before spitting out her words.

"Yes, *that.*" She takes a step back and pops her hip to the side, arms crossed for good measure. "You don't take things seriously. You don't have any plans for your life, and you don't care enough to follow the rules. How am I supposed to work with you?"

"I don't know, Kell," I say and slowly approach, closing the space between us again. She looks up at me, wide-eyed and red-cheeked like she thinks I might kiss her—like she thinks she might let me. I stop when I'm close enough to see the tiny specks of green in her eyes. "I guess the same way I'm supposed to work with someone who has a stick up their ass because they live by an unrealistic set of rules and they can't stand not being in control." Her jaw drops, and she's gobsmacked for once. "Catch ya later, Kellyn," I say and turn to walk away with a smile on my face.

"Hey! Where are you going?" she yells.

"Going home to change and take out the piercing. You know where to find me if you want to work…or play." I look over my shoulder to see her fuming mad. Her cheeks are sunburn-red, and she clutches that file folder like her life depends on it.

❊ ❊ ❊

When I get back to the grill, sans lip ring and wearing red, Morgan raises an eyebrow. "What was that all about?" she asks as she refills the fork holder.

"Oh, nothing. Wore the wrong shirt, no facial piercings in food service, blah, blah, blah." I tug her pink-streaked ponytail as I walk by. Morgan's chill as long as Dane isn't around, and since his main gig is working the arcade, she's usually tolerable when we work together.

"Private escort to the boss's office for dress code violations? Man, they're really cracking down this season."

I walk behind the counter and reach for a sleeve of cups from the top shelf. "Yeah, well…you know Kellyn. She's always leading some kind of crusade."

Morgan joins me on the service side of the register and leans back against the counter, folding down a small cardboard box. "Kinda thought there might be something going on between you two," she says and wiggles her eyebrows.

"Riiiight."

"You know it wouldn't be the worst thing, Vin. Someone like her might be good for you."

I stack the cups next to the ice machine and shake my head. Like I'd ever take advice from a girl whose relationship status changes by the minute. "I don't know what you're talking about," I say. "We're as different as night and day except for one thing."

"Oh yeah, what's that?" Morgan asks.

"We can't stand each other."

LITTLE MISS GIGGLES

Friday, May 22, 2009: Kellyn

"I can't stand him!" I growl and shove the storage tub back into the closet with unnecessary force. Merren laughs, shaking her head as she cuts shapes out of construction paper.

"This is funny to you?" I ask, joining her at the table.

"You're just so worked up over it, Kell. It's kind of telling."

"Uh, yeah. I'm telling you he's a pain in the ass."

She hands me a stack of blue paper and scissors. "Stars, please."

I start on my task but continue to fume. "How does she expect me to get anything done with him slowing me down? It's like she wants me to fail."

"Well, I don't know if that's true, but maybe she thinks you're up for the challenge," Merren says, gathering her paper scraps into a pile and sweeping them into the trash bin she has pulled up beside her. "If anything, it probably means she has faith in you. She knows you can pull it off even with Vinny slowing you down."

I know what she's doing. She's trying to be the voice of reason in my little hissy fit. I don't want to admit she's right, but I guess there could be *some* truth to it. If my mom didn't have any faith in me, there's no way she'd put Vinny on the project, too. That would guarantee a disaster, and she'd never want that for Sweetwater.

Ugh, fine! With one last snip of the scissors, I drop the blue stars onto the table like oversized confetti. "I gotta get over to the gift shop," I say, standing up and pushing the chair back in place. "See ya later at the apartment."

❋ ❋ ❋

After three hours of greeting guests, ringing up their orders, and answering questions with a Sweetwater smile, the clock finally hits eight, and I tidy up the merchandise for the morning. I'm starving, so I figure I'll grab a bite at the grill and see if Vinny is ready to work on the festival. Whenever I had a free moment or the gift shop traffic was slow, I flipped through the file folder and made a few notes. Now I'm ready to dive in and start checking things off the list.

The sunset paints the sky pink as I pull up to the grill and park the golf cart between two others. A handful of customers are scattered around the dining area, eating burgers and nachos, but no one is at the counter. I scoot past the register and find Morgan prepping a burger, while JT pulls out a fresh batch of fries. "Hey, can I get in on that?" My mouth is watering already.

"Sure, Kell. Whatcha having?" JT asks with a wink.

"Whatever's easiest for you guys." I look around for Vinny, who's *supposed* to be working right now. "Aren't you a little understaffed?"

"Nah, Vinny was here but had to split early. Something to do with a chick, I think," JT says.

That son of a bitch.

"You good, there, Kell?" Morgan asks, and I hope I didn't say what I was thinking out loud.

"Yeah–you guys want some help? I can start cleanup or…"

"I think we're good." JT walks toward me, holding out a red basket of fries.

I take it and add ketchup. "Thanks. Was it crazy in here tonight?"

"No more than usual," Morgan says, placing three burger patties on buns. "Order up."

"Heard you and Vinny got called into the office. Tsk, tsk, tsk." JT teases with a mischievous grin on his face.

"Thanks, Morgan," I say, taking one of the burgers and adding condiments as I ignore JT's comment, but he sidles up to me at the prep counter.

"Did mommy find out?" he asks quietly. I give him a jab with my elbow. Unfortunately, JT knows about my epic mistake with his best friend, and he likes to give me shit about it whenever he can.

I carry my basket of food to the other side of the galley and lean against the counter as I eat my meal, sticking my tongue out at JT when he wiggles his eyebrows at me. The guests clear out of the dining area, one table at a time, and I overhear their plans for tomorrow—swimming, going down to the lake, and, of course, the summer kickoff party. I love seeing their excitement for what we've built here.

When I finish eating and clean up my mess, I add my order to the staff ticket in the cash drawer. "Sure you don't need any help with cleanup?" I ask, but they refuse my offer again, so I head back out to the golf cart. The pink sunset sky has melted into dusk, and a sweet honeysuckle kiss teases the air.

I drive over to Vinny's, but honestly, he could be anywhere. I'm not looking forward to seeing this *chick* he's hooking up with tonight—in fact, I'd rather not be here at all, but I'm not going to let him fuck up my project.

Parking the golf cart by my brother's truck on the shared gravel drive, I grab the file folder and walk across the lawn to Vinny's unit. With a deep breath, I remind myself that I'm not interested and I don't give a fuck who he's with. Then I pound on the door.

A moment later, the door opens, and Teak stands on the other side. "Oh, hey, Kellyn!" He's smiling ear-to-ear and steps closer to hug me. He smells like weed.

"Okay, there, buddy. Is Vinny here?" Untangling myself from his embrace, I step into the apartment and hear laughter coming from one of the bedrooms off the hall.

"Vinny!" Teak shouts, taking my hand and tugging me along after him through the apartment and toward the laughter. When he stops, we're standing at the open doorway to a hazy disaster of a bedroom, where some tiny blonde chick sits on a bed, laughing hysterically. Guess he has a type. *Asshole.*

"Uh-oh," she says when her eyes fall on me. "Someone's in trouble." The cackling starts up again, and I hope it's the weed and not just her personality.

Vinny's leaning against the wall across from the doorway, his red resort polo untucked and his dark hair tousled in the sexiest damn way. "You need something?" he asks as if he has no idea why I'm here. Then he takes a hit of the joint between his fingers.

Fuck this. I'm not chasing his ass around the resort and waiting for him to take this seriously. I turn to leave, which sends little Miss Giggles into another fit of laughter. Kicking beer cans, pieces of clothing, and a random beach ball out of the way, I make it to the front door without any followers, which just pisses me off even more. *Fuckin' Vinny.*

When I step outside, I hear my brother's voice and look over to his side of the apartment unit. He's with Merren, and they're standing on the passenger side of his truck bed, getting closer as they talk. *The actual fuck?* I'm not ready to confront that nightmare, so I turn to go back inside the apartment and run smack into Vinny.

"So, what are you here for, Boss?" he asks, placing his hands on my arms to steady me.

"Wha–"

"Work or play?"

I'm so fucking flustered, I can't even think. Then I hear Giggles going another round inside the apartment. "Work. *Obviously.*" I step out of his hold with maybe an extra ounce or two of dramatic flair. But he just smiles and walks backward into the apartment, holding the door open for me.

"What?" I ask because he's just standing there, smiling at me, and it's fucking unnerving.

"Let's work."

"Seems like you're a little busy with your guest at the moment."

Vinny laughs and looks over his shoulder. "I think Teak's got it covered."

I peek around the corner to see if the coast is clear of my best friend and my brother, but it's not. Fuck. Guess I'm going in.

"Whatever. You better be serious about this. I'm not in the mood," I say, stomping past him.

"You got it, Boss," he says and closes the door behind me. I look at the small table in the kitchen area—it's covered with junk. The couch and coffee table are even worse.

"How can you guys live like this? I can't even think right now." I feel myself becoming overwhelmed and agitated. Everything is chaos and anarchy. It's so Vinny.

"We can work upstairs," he says and starts walking toward the hallway. I follow him and when we pass the bedroom he was in earlier, I notice the laughing has died down. The door is shut now, and I don't see Teak anywhere—wonder how I missed Giggles' exit.

As I follow him up the stairs, I catch a glimpse of his boxers peeking out where his jeans hang a little lower on his ass, and it reminds me of that night on the dock. *Fuckin' Vinny.* I purposely slow down to put space between us and stare at my sneakers, taking each step.

At the top of the landing, he flips on the light, and I'm shocked to see a room that's clean. I can actually see the floor, and the bed is made. I don't even know what to think.

"Don't act so surprised," he says and walks over to sit down on the bed, which is just a mattress on the carpeted floor. Then it hits me, this is *his* room. Before tonight, I'd only been in the living room of their apartment. The three times we hooked up last year, it was always somewhere else.

"This is your room?" I ask. "I thought you... Downstairs with..."

He shakes his head, wearing a self-satisfied smile. "So it bothered you, huh? Interesting."

"The only thing that bothered me was the complete absence of anything resembling order."

"If you say so." He smirks and pats the spot next to him on the bed. "Are we gonna work or not?"

MY ASS IS YOURS

Saturday, May 22, 2009: Vinny

She's so flustered, it's hot. She just can't stand being wrong, or maybe it's more that she can't stand it when *I'm* the one who proves her wrong. Yeah, our apartment is a wreck—you've got three guys living here, what do you expect? But, whether Kellyn believes it or not, I know how to be responsible. I just don't get my panties in a twist over every fucking thing like she does.

She doesn't join me on the bed but sits cross-legged on the floor in front of me, spreading papers from the file folder all around, and each one has about five Post-it notes sticking to it. Shit, I'm in for a long night.

"I looked over the details and put together a prioritized list of what we need to do." She hands me a paper with boxes and bullet points. "It's not great. I didn't have a chance to type it up, but hopefully, you can read my handwriting."

I look over the paper, *front and back*. "You forgot something... I don't see breathing on the list."

"Is everything a joke to you?" she asks, all high and mighty.

"At least I can take a joke," I say and set the paper aside. She follows the paper with her eyes and then snaps them back at me.

"We're not done with that."

I scoot off the bed, leaving her precious paper behind, and join her on the floor, close enough to smell the trace of her perfume that lingers after a long day. "Look, we both know how this is going to go." I take a strand of hair that's fallen out of her ponytail and tuck it behind her ear.

Her eyes widen just so and a hint of pink touches her cheeks. "Wha–"

"You're gonna tell me what to do and when to do it. Then you're gonna tell me how I did it wrong and make me do it again. I don't need a list because you won't let me forget. So just tell me what you want me to do, Boss."

Her blue eyes are a storm of irritation and desire, just like that first night last year. God, it turns me on. She's struggling right now—fighting herself for control, but she won't break. Not yet.

"Fine," she says and gathers her spread of papers into the folder. "Like my mom said, Tyler will be here tomorrow to check out the space, and as much as I hate to admit it, I need you there to answer his technical questions. I didn't have time to do a deep dive into the resort's electrical capacity and generators. So, make sure you know that shit, I guess."

"Done. What else?"

She lets out a little huff as she flips through her novel-length stack of papers and flutters her eyelashes in a way that tells me she's annoyed. "The stage," she says. "I've never been part of the team that assembles it, but I'm guessing you have." I nod and try to contain my amusement at how much this is bothering her.

"Right, so I guess you can handle the stage..." She unclips a pen from the file folder and scribbles something down.

"You got it, Boss," I say, and Kellyn's eyes dart to mine.

"Why do you keep calling me that? I'm not the boss."

"Aren't you?" I ask, inching closer to her—close enough to kiss her if I thought she'd go for it. She's considering it. I can tell by the way her breathing picks up and she pulls her brows together just a little bit. When she swallows and her lips part to inhale, a loud thud crashes through the silence, and she jerks her head over her shoulder to look toward the stairs. A second later, we hear them laughing—Teak and his date. The tension has snapped, and Kellyn stands up, tucking the file folder under her arm.

"The rest is on the list. Just try to knock some of those things out as soon as you can. I'll get out of your hair so you can get back to your guest," she says with a slight edge. "But if you're serious about this project, you need to keep your nights open. We have a lot to do in a short amount of time. You can have all the giggly fun you want *after* the festival."

I stand up and follow her to the stairs, not even trying to hide the smile on my face. "You got it, Boss. My ass is yours."

May 23, 2009

Just before two, I remove my apron and hang it on the hook by the back door. "Catch ya at the set up later," I tell JT as I walk by and thank him again for covering for me.

I hop in my golf cart and drive past families heading to and from the pool, sun hats, goggles, and towels in tow. The line for the ice cream shoppe is growing long as it typically does around this time of day, and kids are gathering at the playground where Merren leads a scavenger hunt.

When I reach the Great Lawn, I expect to find Kellyn stomping her foot impatiently, but she's not around. Instead, I find Mrs. Daniels talking to a guy with a clipboard—the festival contact, I assume. I make my way toward them, and when Mrs. Daniels notices, she waves me over, and I pick up the pace.

"Vinny, this is Tyler Harlow, the festival liaison," she says as I approach.

"Nice to meet you. Vinny Moretti," I say, extending my hand to shake his. It's a decent handshake. I respect that. He looks like he could have been a cool guy five or ten years ago. Now, what's left of his rocker persona is choking to death under a button-down and khakis and shoes that cost twice what I make in a month, but I guess that's corporate America—turning rebels into robots.

"Vinny is the assistant to our groundskeeper, so you're in good hands with him," Mrs. Daniels says. "Our other festival coordinator will be here shortly, but I'm needed back at the main office, so I'll let you two get started." She gives me an encouraging pat on the back as she walks away,

42

and I scan the area for Kellyn again. Still no sign of her. She's gonna be pissed as hell.

"So, Vinny, have any experience with music festivals?" Tyler asks, pulling my focus back on the meeting.

"Some. I used to be in a band, and we played a few festivals." In one second, his entire mood changes, like I just passed the secret handshake test and we're bros now.

"Right on, right on. What did you play?"

"Guitar," I say and look over my shoulder for Kellyn. "You play?"

He shakes his head. "Not guitar, no. Drums were always my thing, but now I'm on the business side of the industry. All the perks of being with the band, plus a steady paycheck, and hanging out with guys like Zac Brown, Uncle Kracker…"

I can tell he's the kind that would be fine standing here, name-dropping bands and bigwigs, but I'd rather just get this meeting over with. I still have to face Kellyn and whatever storm she rides in on, showing up late, plus we have to prep for the summer kickoff party tonight. "Right, so…what questions do you have about the setup?"

Tyler opens the storage component of his clipboard and pulls out a sheet of paper, handing it to me. "These are our electrical requirements, but keep in mind, this only covers stage lights, sound, and band needs."

I look over the notes and do some calculations in my head. "Not a problem. We can handle this. What about—"

"I'm so sorry I'm late. Thank you for your patience," Kellyn says, bustling over in a huff. "I'm Kellyn, and this is Vinny. We're the resort's festival coordinators, and we're here to make sure everything you need is ready to go for the event."

Tyler's focus is entirely on Kellyn now. I've faded into the background with the shrubbery as far as he's concerned. Kellyn's babbling on and clutching the damn file folder to her chest like a toddler holding their blankie. Tyler closes in on her—almost a mirror image, hugging his clipboard and looking down at her with greedy eyes and a smile that's already affecting her. My God, she needs a bib to catch her drool.

"Great to meet you, Kellyn. Your partner and I were just going over the electrical requirements."

Kellyn's gooey-eyed gaze is knocked off its track when she hears that. Now she's giving me a salty look. "Fantastic," she says with a fake smile aimed my way. "That's one thing we can check off the list."

"Oh, speaking of lists…" Tyler pulls a set of papers from the clipboard and hands them to Kellyn. "This is a breakdown of what we'll need. I like to give this to the site coordinator as early as possible—really helps us avoid major snags and holdups."

Shit, he's her twin.

Kellyn gushes over the list and prides herself on having addressed some of the tasks already. While she's getting off on Tyler's organizational skills, I catch his eyes crawling all over her body, and hell, it's not like I blame him, but still, dude—chill the fuck out.

Their conversation becomes more exclusive as they walk to different parts of the Great Lawn, visually mapping out the event. I follow along for a while, but it's clear they don't need my help. I doubt they even see me outside their little love bubble made of Post-it notes, paper clips, and bullet-point lists.

"Right, well I'm gonna head back to the grill…" I say, walking backward away from them and fighting the knot in my gut. I don't do jealousy. I don't get attached to girls I've only hooked up with a few times, and I don't do relationships, so what the fuck is happening right now?

PATRON SAINT OF OBEDIENCE

Saturday, May 23, 2009: Kellyn

"Did you pick up the glow sticks?" Merren asks, looking through tub after tub of party supplies that have taken over the cinema.

"They should be in a cardboard box," I say, trying to remember where I put them. "Over there, maybe?" I point to the back side of the room where the concession stand and restrooms sit at the top of the sloping floor. Our little cinema is a guest favorite. It's small and a little outdated, but it's full of memories and charm.

"Found them!" Merren's hand shoots up from the mess of boxes with a glow stick bouquet like the Statue of Liberty's torch. "Guess some got activated in the move. Here." She hands me a pink glow stick that I wrap around my wrist to form a bracelet. She does the same with a green one that's already glowing and hands me three more. "So when do I get to meet him?"

My nerves flutter at the thought of Tyler. "Hopefully tonight. He said he'd be here to check out the optics and sound."

"What does he look like? And don't say gorgeous this time, give me specifics," Merren says with a laugh as she gathers bubble solution, the glow sticks, and miniature beach balls into a wagon.

"Okay, well, he's taller than me–"

"Who isn't?"

"Fair point. He has dark hair, kinda shaggy, like obviously musician vibes you know? And his teeth are perfect. I wouldn't be surprised if he was raised by a dentist. He has this great smile, just so full of confidence, and– oh, did I tell you I saw part of a neck tattoo peeking out from under his shirt?"

"Sounds yummy," Merren says and motions for me to hold the door as she pulls the wagon outside.

"So yummy." I follow her to the kiddie table she's setting up for the party. Guests are already gathered on the Great Lawn, staking their spots for the outdoor movie. Camper chairs and picnic blankets pop up every few minutes now.

"Hey," Kade says as he walks up beside me. "Mom's trying to find you."

I look in the direction he came from and see Tyler chatting with my parents. Damn, he looks good with my family. "Be back in a minute, Mer," I tell her and scoot through the gathering crowd to meet him.

"Oh, here she is," my mom says. "Tyler has some questions about the lighting and sound equipment we're using tonight. I haven't seen Vinny around, so I thought maybe you could help him."

Oh, sure, mom. Love that I'm your second choice in the matter. But, okay… I'm not entirely confident I'll be able to answer his questions. Motioning for him to follow, I walk toward the sound table.

"Wow, this is quite a party you guys are throwing," Tyler says as we make our way across the lawn. I scan the crowd for Vinny, who *should* be wearing the resort's 2009 shirt but probably isn't. I can't find him anywhere. Typical.

"Yeah, the guests love it. They come back for it every year."

We come up on Merren at the kiddie table, and Kade is still hanging around. Be more obvious, guys. "Merren," I say, pulling Tyler along. "This is Tyler Harlow. Tyler, this is my best friend and roommate, Merren McGrath."

"I've heard so much about you," Merren says and I just about die.

"Already?" Tyler laughs, shifting his eyes from Merren to me. Kill me now.

"She's kidding. Big joker," I say, shooting her a look. "And this is my stalker brother, Kade. He won't leave us alone even though he has work to do somewhere else, I'm sure."

"Right, Kade," Tyler says with a nod. "We met earlier." He looks at his watch and then turns to me. "So about the lights and–"

"Of course. Right over here." I lead the way as we cut through the crowd, and when we make it to the other side, I see Vinny. With a girl. At the sound table. And wouldn't you know it, the fucker's wearing the right damn shirt this time.

Tyler starts talking tech as we approach, but I don't even try to comprehend—in part because I have no fucking idea what any of it means, but more so because irrational frustration and anger have hijacked my system. This chick must be illiterate because she clearly cannot read the "employees only past this point" sign.

Charging toward the cozy couple, I clear my throat to get their attention. "I'm sorry, Miss, but I'm going to have to ask you to leave. As the sign clearly says, employees only. It's for your safety." The girl, who's sitting on Vinny's lap, long dark hair flowing over her suntanned shoulders, looks at him with a sad puppy dog look. *Are you fucking serious?* I can't hear what they're saying, and fuck if I want to, but they're laughing and she's whispering in his ear now and in no hurry to vacate the area.

"Vinny!" I slam my hands down on the sound table, which finally garners a reaction from him. "You're on the clock. Save your little weekly flings for your own time. Tyler needs to talk to you."

Poor girl doesn't like being referred to as a fling and gives me a dirty look as she removes herself from Vinny's lap. *Bye, bitch.*

As Tyler walks around to the other side of the sound table, I catch Vinny staring at me, but he doesn't look irritated at all considering I just delivered a successful cock block. No—that self-satisfied little smirk of his tugs at the corner of his mouth, his lip ring like a fucking comma. Asshole.

My death glare is broken when Tyler sits down beside Vinny and starts asking him questions. With a huff, I turn and walk away to find Merren, silently chiding myself for getting worked up back there. The hell was that about? Shake it off, Kellyn. I breathe in the Sweetwater air—the perfect blend of fresh-cut grass, lakeside breeze, and honeysuckle. This is home to me.

With more composure than I had two minutes ago, I smile gracefully at the guests I encounter along the way. The lawn games are in full swing with potato sack races and hula hoop contests to my left and a corn hole tournament starting on my right. The sun is sinking into a pink and purple sky, and soon it'll be showtime.

Back at the kiddie table, Merren helps our younger guests with their glow stick bracelets and bubble wands. The little kids always lose interest in the film, so we like to offer them other ways to stay entertained while their parents enjoy the movie.

"Where's Tyler?" Merren asks when I sit down beside her and start handing out bubble wands to the line of kids.

"Talking to Vinny about tech stuff. Where's Kade?"

She stops in the middle of hooking a bracelet on a little girl's wrist and turns to me. "How should I know?"

Okay, we're still playing secrets. Got it.

By the sun's last goodnight, the Great Lawn is alive with the excited hum of guests settling in with popcorn and candy, ready to watch Baby take the stage. Little kids with glow stick bracelets flutter around like fireflies in the dusk, and a countdown projected onto the screen begins. As the crowd quiets to a murmur, the cicada song adds to the ambiance and I look for Tyler. Surely he's done talking shop with Vinny by now.

Just as I'm turning around to go find him, I spot Tyler walking over. "Hey, I was about to come to find you," I say, hurrying to meet him. "Guess you guys got it all sorted out?"

"Oh yeah, everything's looking good. I'll stop by next week to go over the last-minute details. You have my cell if anything comes up, but you guys seem to have it under control," he says and starts to walk away.

"You're leaving?"

He backtracks two steps. "Well, yeah... I got what I came for," he says, and I'm crushed. Completely. I thought he was flirting with me earlier, and when I mentioned the movie tonight, he seemed interested, but I guess he was only interested in the tech equipment.

"Is there something else?" he asks, tilting his head and finding my eyes.

"No...not for the festival. I just thought you might want to stick around and watch the movie," I say and hear just how pathetic I sound. This guy is gorgeous and mature and has his shit together—why would he want to watch an old eighties flick with me and a hundred strangers?

Tyler steps closer, but only our shadows touch under the outdoor lighting. "I'd love to, Kellyn..." I look up at him with hope for half a second and understand there's a *but* coming. "I have a lot on my plate right now, and I just can't take the night off," he says and reaches for my hand. "But I really wish I could."

I nod, feeling slightly less rejected by the warmth of his touch. "I understand."

"But, hey, do you have plans Memorial Day? Some buddies and I are taking a boat out... You wouldn't want to come with, would you?"

"I'd love to, Tyler. That sounds amazing," I gush and then try to play it cool. "I mean, yeah… I think I can make that work."

He flashes those pearly whites. "Great, I'll give you a call later," he says, giving my hand a quick squeeze before letting go and walking away.

I want to squeal and kick my feet and tell Merren I have a date with Tyler, but she's leading a quiet game of hot potato with a group of kids… and Kade, her new "assistant," apparently. So, I hurry off to the gazebo at the far end of the Great Lawn. If I'm lucky and no couple has claimed it, I can still watch the film from there, away from the crowd.

When I reach the vacant gazebo I, climb the bench to sit on the railing and watch as Baby and Johnny's dancing heats up the screen. Tyler has some Swayze-like features…the jawline, I think…and his eyes. Hell, the longer I watch the film, the more similarities I find. And just as I'm imagining the rest of that neck tattoo, I lose my balance—no, I'm *pulled* backward—and nearly fall off the railing.

"What do we have here?" Vinny says, his hands on my waist, steadying me back onto the railing.

"Vinny! You fucking jerk, I could have fall–"

"No, you couldn't have because I had you the whole time," he says and hops over the railing to sit beside me.

"Why aren't you at the sound table?" I ask, crossing my arms and scooting an inch away from him.

"JT's shift. Why aren't you following Tyler around?"

"He left. Where's the flavor of the week?"

"American Hi-Fi? That's the best you got?" He laughs and runs his hands through his already messy hair. I hop off the railing but he follows close behind. "Why do you care anyway?" he asks, and I spin around to face him, attempting my most convincing defense.

"I don't care as long as she's not breaking the rules."

"God, Kellyn. You and your rules. I've never met anyone so obsessed with rules. You're like the patron saint of obedience."

"It's not *my* rule. She was in a restricted area. *Employees only.* It was for her safety. It's a liability—"

"Yeah the liability was you pulling her hair and dragging her out of there," Vinny says, topping it off with that fucking smug little smirk of his. It takes everything in me not to explode. I clench my toes and jaw and fists and turn to walk away because if I stay here one more second, I'll either kill him or kiss him, dammit.

❈ ❈ ❈

It's almost midnight by the time we get home from breaking down the party. After changing into my PJs, I toss my dirty clothes in the hamper and join Merren at the bathroom sink.

"Where'd you run off to? Somewhere cozy with Tyler?" she asks through a mouthful of toothpaste.

"Psh. I wish," I say, taking a makeup wipe and running it over my face. "He had to leave early. I ended up watching the movie from the gazebo."

"Alone?" she asks with a knowing look.

I toss the wipe in the trash can in the corner. "Unfortunately not."

Merren spits, rinses, gargles, and spits again. "How'd that go?" She wiggles her eyebrows up and down.

"What are you on? It was intolerable. I was trying to enjoy the movie in peace, and along comes Vinny to fuck it all up as usual."

She laughs. That's it. She doesn't defend me or bash Vinny for being the annoying asshole that he is. She just laughs. "What the hell is so funny, Mer?" I ask as she walks past me and into the hallway.

"You and Vinny. The way he gets under your skin and you get all hot and bothered, but you're oblivious to the fact that it's happening. It's comical," she says, now facing me as she leans on the doorway to her room.

"Hot and bothered?" I repeat her comprehensively inaccurate words. "Oh, no. I'm *not* hot and bothered. I'm just fucking annoyed."

Mer crosses her arms and tilts her pretty little head as she gives me the smile she doles out on the kids in the activity center. "And why do you think that is?"

I scoff at the ridiculousness of her question. "Because he's fucking annoying."

"Mmm." She shakes her head. "You seem to be the minority in that opinion."

"What, did you take a poll?"

"No, but I don't find him annoying, and everyone else gets along with him. JT, Teak, Morgan, Kade—"

"Fine. Whatever," I say just to shut down her "In Praise of Vinny" soliloquy. "He's like the complete opposite of me, and I can't stand that. At all."

"You know what they say about opposites…"

"They kill each other?" I patronize her. I'm over this inquisition.

"Well maybe if they don't fuck first," Mer says with a laugh.

I roll my eyes so hard it hurts and feel my cheeks turning red, dammit. "You're so off base."

"Am I?" She reaches toward me, tickling my waist as I walk past her to my bedroom door. I try to dodge her but fail, so I go for the back of her knee, where I know she'll buckle immediately. And she does. We're tangled up on the floor, a bundle of laughter and shrieks, both knowing each other's weak spots and not afraid to use them.

"Okay, okay—" I say as I try to catch my breath and gain the upper hand. "Peace?"

Merren freezes, like she's thinking about it, then relaxes. "Peace," she says and loosens her hold on me.

A few stray laughs make their way out as we lie here, staring at the popcorn ceiling, catching our breath. "Mer… Would you say I'm the patron saint of obedience?"

"Yes, sweetie, and we love you for it."

MY LADY KELLYN OF
SWEETWATER SUN AND SPORT

Sunday, May 24, 2009: Vinny

Sundays at Sweetwater are usually insane. The main office is packed with guests checking out; housekeeping is running around like crazy trying to turn rooms for the new wave of check-ins at two; and by four, the line starts to form for the Sunday evening buffet at the main house. It's so popular that it draws townies and the lakehouse elite in addition to the resort guests. It's a full house and then some. But today's turnover is little to none, being Memorial Day weekend, so even though it doesn't seem like it would be, today is a low-key day for the staff. The evening buffet rush will still be intense, but we have all day to prepare for that madness.

I catch Teak on the way out the door when I get downstairs. "Where you headed?" I holler and catch up with him.

"Told Matty I'd take her riding before the stables open."

Matty Cole is the groundskeeper's daughter and has been adopted as a little sister by most of the staff. She's only fifteen, but she's a smart kid and one of the sweetest people I've met. Like me, she lives here year-round, so we have a closer sibling-like relationship than some of the others.

"Have fun–but Teak, don't let her fall off this time, man," I tell him as we go our separate ways.

I pull out my phone to look at the time. It's not even eight-thirty yet, and I have three—*three*—text messages from Kellyn. For fuck's sake, does she ever sleep? "Catch ya later," I say as we step outside and Teak heads off to the stables.

I hop in the golf cart and open the first message, received at six o'clock on the dot.

Lots of work to do today. Meet at 8. Great Lawn.

Seeing as it's a quarter past eight and I'm still in front of my place, I know exactly what Kellyn looks like right now—scowl pulling at her little sun-kissed face, dark blue eyes all squinty and fierce, and her pouty little mouth holding back all the obscenities she'll unleash on me the second I show up.

I move to the next message, received an hour later.

Actually, I'm free now. Just come asap.

Oh shit. I laugh. She's been waiting for over an hour? I'm surprised she didn't beat down the door and drag me out of bed. I start the golf cart and read the latest message, received three minutes after eight.

That was 8 AM...in case I didn't make myself clear.

Yep, gonna be a hell of a Sunday. I back out and race over to the Great Lawn, though race isn't an accurate description considering I have to contend with guests, other golf carts, housekeeping mini trucks, and a few guest vehicles here and there.

When I pull up, she's already marching toward me, fuse lit and about to explode. "Why do you even have a phone if you're not going to check it?" she shouts, waving her cell around and attracting the attention of a few guests passing by.

I meet her halfway and check my phone for the time. "It's just now eight-thirty–"

"And I've been here since seven!"

I hold up my cell with a hint of arrogance, and I know I shouldn't, but it's so easy to knock her off that damn high horse of hers. Hell, it's fun too. "But you told *me* to be here at eight," I say.

"And you weren't." She whips herself around and starts to walk away, but I grab her by the hand, and she turns to face me as I drop to one knee over dramatically.

"From the deepest caverns of my dark and twisted heart, I beg your merciful and unequaled forgiveness, my lady, Kellyn of Sweetwater Sun and Sport."

Looking up at her, the sun casts a halo over that crazy little blonde head of hers, and I notice how the blue resort polo she's wearing is almost the same shade as her eyes, but not nearly as beautiful.

She snaps her hand away and leaves me scrambling to my feet as she storms off in a huff. "Oh, c'mon, Kell. I'm just messing around."

When I catch up to her, she turns around and slams the file folder against my chest. "That's the problem, Vinny. You're *always* messing around. This is serious. This is work. This is why I didn't want to work with you in the first place."

"What—because you knew I'd show up thirty minutes late? It's not the end of the world." I open the folder to look at her newly typed notes, color-coordinated with footnotes and everything.

"Tyler and I have a plan—a schedule to follow. While you were off messing around and sleeping in, the grown-ups did the prep work."

"Hold up, I wasn't messing around or sleeping in. You didn't even tell me I needed to be here until this morning. That's poor planning on your part—"

She charges toward me, but I put my hands up in peace and back away slowly. "And *grownups*? Really, Kellyn? You're younger than me. Or are you referring to Tyler and your parents because they're in the same age bracket, I bet."

"I may be younger but I'm a hell of a lot more mature than you are, and Tyler isn't even close to my parents' age. Maybe you should get your eyes checked."

I look up from Kellyn's Guide to Micromanaging a Music Festival and leisurely follow her petite frame with my eyes, taking extra time to appreciate how those little white shorts hug her hips and thighs and the way her early summer tan looks even darker in contrast to the fabric.

"Hello? What's your problem—"

"Nothing. No problem," I say, looking back up to her face. "I was just checking my eyesight. Everything's coming in crystal clear."

"Oh my God, you're a child. Can you just focus on the list, please?" she says and tries to pretend it doesn't affect her when I look at her like that, but she's a horrible liar. It's written all over her face. She's blushing and flitting her eyes everywhere she can to avoid meeting mine.

Looking over the list, I notice every single task is broken down into step-by-step instructions. She probably could have knocked out one or two of these items with the time she spent making the damn thing.

"This is all me?" I ask.

"Yes, that's all *you*... For phase one. I have more–"

"Just how many phases are there?"

"Tyler and I broke it down into three phases for best practices and–"

I'm howling with laughter and she looks like she wants to slug me. "I'm sorry," I say, trying to bottle it up as I clutch the file folder to my chest in defense and back away from her death glare that could probably slice through my soul. "I'm sorry. Look, it's just...*three phases*? Can we at least take this inside? I don't want to get heatstroke."

❈ ❈ ❈

After convincing Kellyn to get out of the heat, we—and by *we,* I mean *she*—decided to continue our meeting in the golf cart garage. There's no AC, but it's out of the sun and there are a couple big shop fans. Taking a Sharpie from the old beat-up desk in the corner, I start crossing items off my list, rewriting some of her instructional notes, and even drawing a couple arrows to change the order of her plans.

"What the fuck, Vinny," she says when she sees my handiwork. "You just–you just–" Kellyn looks at me wide-eyed and angry. "Do you know how much time I spent on that?"

"No, but probably too much." I brush past her as I walk to the far end of the garage, and soon she's yipping at my heels.

When I open the door that connects to the maintenance barn and start to walk through, she grabs the back of my shirt and pulls. "What are you doing?"

"Items three-hundred through four-twenty-eight, I think." Holding the door open, I wait for her to pass, and once she's safely beyond the door's swing, I let it slam back in place, the echo bouncing off the high metal ceiling.

With my list and Sharpie in hand, I make my way up and down the aisles of shelving and equipment, checking boxes as I go. Behind me, she's going on about the phases, the time crunch, the pressure, and all the ways I'm slowing her down. It's just noise. She's like a tea kettle winding up her whistle.

"Vinny!" she yells when I don't respond. "Do you hear me?"

"Trying hard not to," I say, turning around to face her. "Why are you doing this?"

She starts to lay into me again, but I step closer and put my index finger on her lips, silencing her for once. "You let things become so big in

61

your mind, Kell... It doesn't have to be that way." The rise and fall of her chest picks up the longer we touch, her eyes wide and stormy like lightning on the lake, and I'm afraid she might bite my finger clear off.

"Why can't you just breathe? Just let it be?" I ask, lowering my finger out of biting range—I hope—and resting my hand on her shoulder. She shrugs, and I'm not sure if it's a response to my question or an attempt to remove my touch.

"You can do it, you know. I've seen you do it." I watch her eyes follow my thumb as I run it across the pique cotton sleeve of her polo. "When you were with me," I say, and shift my weight so I'm the slightest bit closer to her. "You let go of everything, Kell. You *lived* in the moment. You can't tell me you didn't love that feeling because I was right there, living it with you."

She raises her eyes to mine, and I see her—for the first time since last summer, I see *her*—the Kellyn I can't get out of my head or dirty dreams. *Fuck it.* I'm gonna kiss her. I move my hand from her shoulder to cradle her head just behind her ear and—Fuck!—her damn phone rings, and like a magic spell, it wakes her from this reality.

"Hello?" She holds the phone to her ear as she slowly backs away from me. *It's Tyler,* she mouths and points to the cell with her free hand. Fanfuckingtastic.

"Oh, sure...that sounds great," she says with a flirty giggle that turns my stomach. She's moving farther and farther out of reach, like Tyler's reeling her back to shore. Kellyn points to the list in my hand, then

62

to a nonexistent watch on her wrist, and walks out the door. The slam that follows hits me like the snap of a guitar string, and I remember why I agreed to the hook up in the first place. I never have to worry about the girls that come and go all summer, but someone you see every day, that's a different story—one I lived before and regret. But Kellyn's rules were clear and safe and reasonable: one time, no feelings, no one finds out. Problem is, rules—even good ones—beg to be broken, and fuck it if Kellyn wasn't right —I can't follow the damn things.

THE HELL KIND OF ANTI-APHRODISIAC DID THEY PUT IN THAT FOOD?

Monday, May 25, 2009: Kellyn

I worked my ass off yesterday—with little help from Vinny—and organized the food truck lineup, ordered extra stock for the grill and ice cream shoppe, planned out the parking and shuttle service, and even started on hiring extra security and maintenance staff for the event by reaching out to previous employees. *If* Vinny took care of the items on his list—and that's a very big *if*—we should be ready to start phase two tomorrow. Unfortunately, phase two requires that we work together more than separately. I can already tell I'm going to be exhausted from dealing with him on this next round of tasks, so I'm glad I took the rest of today off to go out with Tyler and his friends.

He's picking me up at five, which means I have about twenty minutes to burn. Merren is working her shift at the gift shop, so I'm home alone and it's killing me to just sit still and do nothing. I pick up my cell and consider checking in with Vinny to make sure he's staying on task, but I decide against it. He'll either ignore my message until later when I'm enjoying my date with Tyler or he'll text back some smart-ass shit that puts me in a bad mood before the date.

Instead, I reach for the file folder that's becoming unusable with wear and transfer the documents to a new sturdier binder, complete with color-coded dividers and tabs. This is my therapy. Structure gives me peace —some people meditate or color to relax, but I organize.

At exactly five o'clock, there's a knock on my door, and I open it to find Tyler in board shorts, a tee shirt, and flip-flops. He flashes a smile made for a toothpaste campaign. "Ready to go?"

I grab my bag and sunglasses and follow him out to his *Escalade?* Damn, he sure cleans up nicely. "Nice ride," I say and settle into the passenger seat.

It's a short drive to the marina, hardly long enough for one song. When we park, Tyler grabs a case of beer from the backseat and leads me down the dock to a beautiful Sunseeker with an elevated deck. This is *not* a boat. This is a fucking yacht. "This is your idea of boating?" I ask him, pulling my sunglasses off for an unrestricted view.

"Nice, huh?" Tyler nudges me, then shifts the pack of beer to his other hand and helps me climb aboard. "The others will be here soon," he says. "Want a tour?"

I position my sunglasses on top of my head and follow him inside the hull. It's stunning—literally stunning—clean and shiny with buttery leather seats surrounding a polished wood table. It's like something out of a movie. Sure, I've seen yachts on the lake before, but I've never been on one myself.

"This way," Tyler says, lugging the pack of beer down a little curved staircase to the galley. He opens the wood-front fridge and places the beer inside to chill. "Through there is a cabin." He points to an open doorway, and I peek inside a bedroom with little space for more than the bed—still, it exudes luxury.

"Bathroom's behind you, and through here..." he says, taking a step down into a narrow corridor, "is the bunk cabin and then the master."

"This is gorgeous, Tyler. I've never been on anything like this." I run my hand along the smooth, shiny wood panels as I step into the master, which is much more spacious than the other cabin.

"Anyone home?" someone hollers from above.

"That'll be Beau and Ciara," Tyler says, taking my hand and leading me back up to the main deck.

The sun is bright and I have to shield my eyes to see them, but Tyler introduces me to a couple who look like they belong here—she's actually wearing a pearl necklace with her bathing suit and sarong. Here I was, thinking I was adequately dressed with a sundress over my bikini, but damn, I forgot my pearls at home.

"Nice to meet you," I tell them as three more strangers and a captain climb aboard. After a round of introductions that leaves my head spinning, Tyler takes me up to the flybridge, where I look out over the dark blue water and inhale the familiar Sweetwater air. "This is quite a view," I say, and turn around to find him sitting at one of the deck tables, looking at his phone.

"Everything okay?" I ask and walk over to him.

"Huh? Oh, yeah. Just a work email. I'm going down to get a drink. Can I get you one?"

"Sure, whatever you're having is fine."

While Tyler is off getting drinks, we push away from the dock, and I text Merren about the yacht, sending her a few pictures from the deck. I put my phone away when I hear voices coming up the stairs. It's Tyler and another guy—Paul or Phil? Tyler hands me a drink, and I take it, sitting down beside him on the bench seat.

"So, Kelly, what is it you do?" Tyler's friend asks, taking a seat across from us.

"Oh, it's Kellyn," I say and laugh it off to ease his embarrassment. "I work at the resort." But his face says he requires more clarification. "Sweetwater Sun and Sport," I say as I motion toward the shore.

"Ahhh," he says and takes a drink of his beer. "Event coordinator or something, right?"

"Something like that. It's my family's business, so I do a little bit of everything." I take a drink—then another—to pass the awkward silence that follows. "Um, I'm sorry, I think I mixed up your names. You're…"

"Phillip," he says with a hint of arrogance that I don't quite understand. He's not nearly as attractive as Tyler, and this isn't even *his* boat.

"Oh, that's right–Phillip. Do you work with Tyler?"

They both laugh like I uncovered an inside joke, but it's lost on me. I take another drink and look out over the water. This isn't quite what I expected when Tyler invited me, but I'm here and Tyler's hot and this boat is fucking fabulous, so I'll just have to find a way to fit in with his friends.

"Damn contacts," I say, cupping my right eye and standing up. "I'll be right back." Tyler nods, and as soon as I reach the stairs, I hear their indistinct conversation start up.

Downstairs, I pass Ciara and Beau and the other two, whose names I can't remember. I find the little closet of a bathroom and lock myself inside. I don't even wear contacts. I just needed a reason to excuse myself. I don't usually have trouble reading people and making friends, but the chemistry was way off with Phillip. Maybe I'll have better luck with Tyler's other friends.

I'm about to leave the bathroom when I hear footsteps coming down the little staircase followed by Tyler's voice. "In the fridge," he says to whoever is with him.

Thinking this could be my opportunity to reset the vibes, I turn the doorknob to leave but freeze when I hear Ciara's voice. "Alright, let's talk about your arm candy, Ty. Did you even check ID?" she asks. Her laughter smothers Tyler's response, and a moment later, their voices fade away. Awesome. Strike two. I know Tyler's older than me—that's part of his appeal—but I'm not *that* much younger, and I've always considered myself mature for my age. Aside from my casual dress, which happens to match

Tyler's perfectly, I can't imagine why Ciara thinks I'm some young piece of *arm candy*.

When I return to the main deck, Tyler and his friends are sitting around the table with their drinks, and I notice that Tyler brought mine down as well. He waves me over to sit beside him. Okay, great, a reset. I can work with this. He places his arm along the seat back behind me and I inch a little closer to him. I try to contribute to the conversation, but every new topic involves bands or musicians I don't know, inside jokes or shared stories I'm not privy to, or work-related tasks that extend beyond the—in Phillip's words—"little resort festival."

This date is a bust, and I'm ready to disembark, but we're not even close to shore. Dinner was mentioned briefly between topics, and I haven't seen any sign of it, so there's still that to get through. Since my drink is almost empty, I finish it off and excuse myself to grab another downstairs.

Below deck, I refill my cup and carry it to the master cabin, where I test out the plush, perfectly made bed. I lie back, holding my drink steady, and stare up at the skylight overhead. I bet it's beautiful when the sky goes dark and the stars come to life. I'll probably be stuck on this boat long enough to see it with my own eyes.

"Whoa, careful there," Tyler says, walking toward me and taking the cup from my hand. "You could have spilled that."

"Oh…" I sit up and smooth my dress over my thighs. "Sorry. I wasn't thinking."

He joins me on the bed, shaking his head as he gives into a smile. "What are you doing in here anyway?"

I shrug and kick my legs out in front of me, wiggling my freshly painted toes. "Didn't really have much to contribute up there, so…"

"Is there something you wanted to contribute?" he asks, and it feels like there's a hint of teasing in the way he says it. Maybe that's his way of flirting. I shift my body to face him.

"How old *are* you?" I ask.

A dry chuckle tumbles from his magazine-perfect smile, and he reaches up to tuck a strand of hair behind my ear. After a thoughtful breath, he says, "I'm twenty-eight."

I let this sink in. Twenty-eight isn't *old*, and it's not like he's thirty yet, but if I do the math, it sounds worse. No. No, this is fine. My dad is five years older than my mom, and that's not weird—what's another four years? It's not like he's ten years older than me… Just nine.

"Still processing?" he asks with a perfectly irresistible little grin.

"I'm fine," I say and reach my hand out to his neck. "What's the tattoo?"

He takes my hand in his, removing it from his neck, and with his other hand, he tugs his shirt down to reveal a phoenix rising from the ashes. "Cliche?"

I shake my head and try to memorize the way my hand feels inside his. "No, I like it."

"Dinner's ready, lovebirds," somebody shouts from up deck, and Tyler releases the neck of his shirt, covering all but a hint of the bird's wings. He stands up, never letting go of my hand, and we return to the table.

❋ ❋ ❋

The meal was an eclectic smorgasbord of highbrow food. I can't even tell you what I ate—could have been octopus, could have been tofu, could have been seaweed. But the mystery meat kept me occupied while Tyler and the others talked shop. It was more boardroom than boat party—guess I should have seen that coming.

After dessert—some fruit-based fancy jello-like situation—I asked Ciara if she wanted to go for a swim, but she laughed it off like it was the most absurd suggestion she'd ever heard. Apparently, her swimsuit is for decoration only. Like me—the arm candy.

Now, I'm back on the flybridge, watching the land grow bigger. We'll dock soon, and I don't know what to expect after that. Maybe Tyler's friends will leave and we can salvage the evening—make it a real date.

"Here you go," Tyler says as he takes the top step and joins me on the upper deck. I accept the drink he holds out and set it on the low table in front of me.

"Oh, coaster," he says and hurries to slide a heavy white square under my drink. I chuckle and sit back against the cushioned bench.

"You're so responsible. It's…refreshing."

"Refreshing?" Tyler laughs. "I guess you hang around a lot of irresponsible people, then?"

"Not by choice." I turn to face him, pulling one leg up under the other. "But you… You're a little hard to figure out."

"In what way?"

"You have this sexy reformed rocker look, but you're super chill and mature and have a handle on life. I mean, you have it all together to the point that you have coasters on your yacht—your *yacht*."

He shrugs, following it with a sheepish smile. I lean closer and trace my fingers over the phoenix wings rising up along his neck. "Then you have this…"

Tyler places his hand over mine, and for a moment, I'm afraid he's going to push it away, but he doesn't. He holds it in place and leans in to kiss me. Finally! This is all I wanted and all I worked for this entire disappointment of an evening. I'm ready for sparks to fly, for fireworks to take over the sky, for my world to explode around me in a kaleidoscope of color.

And when he pulls away, I'm *still* waiting. What the actual fuck? That wasn't a kiss—I mean, it was a kiss, but it wasn't a *kiss*. No. I refuse to accept this. I pull Tyler back to me and try again, and to his credit, he seems to be having a firework moment himself, but no matter how tight I squeeze my eyes or how hard I focus on what I want so badly to feel, it just doesn't happen.

The hell kind of anti-aphrodisiac did they put in that food? The boat jerks as we dock, and I can see that Tyler is calculating his odds of a home run tonight—he's looking pretty confident. Little does he know I threw the game.

"Guess we should go down there," I say and stand slowly. Tyler does the same, taking my hand, and just minutes ago, it was a welcome and promising sensation, but now it's like sticking my hand in a bucket of dead fish. I might actually gag.

Downstairs, we say goodbye to his friends, and after the last one vacates the boat, he pulls me in for a hug. "So... Do you want to stay a little longer?"

I swallow against the nausea and carefully pull away. "I actually have an early shift tomorrow..."

That's all he needs to hear to knock his world off balance. Confusion settles on his face, and I can't blame the guy—I was basically mauling his face minutes ago.

"Sure... I understand," he says, covering his disappointment with a smile. "Another time, maybe."

Thank God the marina is close to the resort because the longer I'm with Tyler, the more nauseous I feel. I really hope this doesn't make things awkward for the festival coming up, but maybe a little distance will clear the repulsion from my system. I'll have to deal with his high hopes later.

As we pass by the main office, I notice a noisy group of swimmers heading to the pool, which is surprising because the pool closed an hour ago. I keep my eyes on them as long as I can, and just before Tyler turns the Escalade and blocks my view, I recognize the leader of the pack. *Fuckin' Vinny.*

LIKE A SEXY LITTLE PARASITE

Monday, May 25, 2009: Vinny

"Late-night pool party!" Teak shouts, throwing himself into the deep end like a cannonball. Three splashes follow, and I lower myself into the hot tub, where JT and two blondes join me. The quiet one—Whitney, I think—sits next to me while the other one floats over to sit on JT's lap. She can't see him faking ecstasy behind her, that dog, but my amusement gives it away, and she turns back to face him just as he shuts it down.

"So, where are you all from?" I ask.

"Stillwater for me," JT's lap girl says. "And Whitney's originally from Kansas. The other three are from Tulsa. What about you guys?"

"Sweetwater born and raised," JT says with pride.

Whitney looks at me, waiting for my response. I scoop bubbling water into my hands, running it over my head and face. "Everywhere," I say.

"Ooh, mysterious," the other one teases and then succumbs to JT's tickling. The frothy water splashes Whitney, and she takes cover, leaning into me. As the ruckus dies down, JT and his girl start kissing—slow at first, then more feverishly. Teak and his crew are playing Marco Polo in the pool, oblivious to the heat wave taking over the hot tub, and under the water, Whitney's hand finds my leg and starts trailing upwards.

I try to get into it, but it's just not happening. I take her hand and hold it to keep her from going any further and embarrassing us both. It's a shame, really. She's fucking hot and clearly willing, but I don't know... She's just not doing it for me tonight—could be stress. Even though I'm not concerned about the festival's success, Kellyn's constant micromanaging is enough to lay seeds of doubt in my mind. It's one thing to know she has zero faith in me and another to hear it on the regular.

When JT comes up for air, he gives me a look as if to ask why I'm not ripping Whitney's bikini off already. I shrug and rest my head against the edge of the hot tub, closing my eyes. The Marco Polo calls grow louder, echoing across the water, and a moment later, I hear Whitney giggle in response to something JT says too quietly for me to make out.

Now she's climbing on my lap, facing me, and running her hands over my chest and shoulders. Any other time, I'd appreciate JT's pitch to get me laid, but tonight, it's a wasted effort. I place my hands on Whitney's waist to remove her from my lap, but she takes it as an invitation to kiss me. Damn, she's a hell of a kisser. Okay, fuck—I'll give it a try. I pull her closer as she slips her tongue against mine, and while I appreciate her skill and commitment to the task, I feel nothing. *Nothing.*

When she pulls away to take a breath, I know it's my chance to shut it down. "Hey, JT," I say. He growls at the interruption. "Can I talk to you for a second?"

"No," he says, his voice muffled against the girl's lips.

I shift Whitney off my lap and try to ease the awkward exchange with a smile. "JT," I say again and clear my throat as I move across the hot tub.

"What?" he whines. Literally whines like a little kid. I smack him on the back of the head and climb out of the hot tub. "Sorry. Be right back," he tells the girls and follows me.

I grab a towel from the shelf near the emergency phone and walk around the corner and out of sight. "What the fuck is your problem, man?" JT asks, returning the smack I gave him.

"I don't know. I'm just... I guess I'm stressed out or something. It's not working for me."

"Are you crazy? She's all over you."

"I'm aware," I say and run the towel back and forth over my head. "Look, I don't want to make it awkward. It's not her, really, she's amazing, but I think I'm gonna head back to–"

"You fucking serious, Vin?" He wipes his face and then shakes his head like a wet dog.

"Yeah, you think you can cover for me? Tell her I'm not feeling good or–I don't know, just tell her something."

"Oh, I'll tell her something, alright. I'll tell her you're a lovesick puppy hung up on someone else." JT grabs the towel from my hands and whips me with it.

"The hell are you talking about man, I'm just stressed about the festival and Kellyn riding my ass."

"Well, you got part of it right," he says and tosses me the towel. "No problem, man, I got you. Good luck with that." JT walks back around the corner, and I wrap the towel around my waist, then slip on my shoes and head back home.

Good luck with that? JT must be smoking something because I'm *not* hung up on anyone, especially Kellyn. She just gets under my skin because she's obsessive and high-strung and has to be up in my business all the damn time. If I were hung up on her, I'd be affected by the fact that she's out on some boat with Tyler right now, but I'm not. Good for her, and God help him.

The resort is quiet as I walk back to the apartment—just the cicadas singing their love songs and the occasional shriek escaping the pool in the distance. When I pass by Kellyn's apartment, the lights are off—she's still out with Tyler, driving him nuts and making his head spin. Lucky bastard.

"Sup, Vinny," Kade hollers from the back of his truck bed as I approach. He's with Merren, which is an unexpected coupling, but who am I to talk? I nod and tell them goodnight, then head inside, kick off my squeaky wet shoes, and drop the damp towel by the front door.

Upstairs, I peel off my wet swim shorts and toss them on the pile of dirty clothes in the corner. The air conditioning feels twice as cold now, and I hurry to find boxers and a tee shirt to put on before I crawl into bed. Lying here, alone in the quiet apartment, my mind takes over the blank canvas of silence, painting memories of last summer with Kellyn. In the hot tub. By the dock. In the empty guest cabin. Fuck. Why won't she leave me alone? I swear, even when she's not around, barking out orders, she still hijacks my mind and body like a sexy little parasite.

I roll onto my stomach and slam a pillow over my head as if that will block it out. I'm in for a long ass night of self-contempt—not for my actions with Whitney tonight or with Kellyn last summer. No, what I hate is that I can't get the fuck over myself and tell her how I really feel and what I want. But the last time I served my heart on a platter, it cost me my band, my dreams, my friends…and, of course, the girl. Tabitha left me so fucked up and alone, I swore I wouldn't go all in for anyone—ever. What are the odds I lose everything if I put myself out there again? Pretty damn good, I bet.

LIKE A FUCKING NUKE OF DESIRE

Tuesday, May 26, 2009: Kellyn

Fucking hell. Another wave of nausea slams into me, and my body revolts. There's nothing left, I want to scream, but I'm too weak and lose the battle to dry heaves again.

"Kell, sweetie, can I get you anything?" Merren asks from the other side of the bathroom door.

"No," I say, my voice amplified by the porcelain throne I cling to. I've been at it all night, and it's almost time to get up for work. There's no way. There's no fucking way. The thought of everything I still have to do for the festival, plus my regular hours, and the impossibility of getting it all done today breaks me, and for the first time in the last six hours, my body exports something other than bile. Tears roll down my clammy face, and then comes the blubbering.

"Oh, Kell, don't cry," Merren says through the door. The sound of my best friend's concern and sympathy overwhelms me, and I give in to sobs. The door opens slowly, and she peeks her head inside, then immediately kneels beside me, wrapping her long, slender arms around the mess that is me.

"Shhh," she hushes me like a baby, rubbing one hand up and down my back and cradling my rat's nest of a head with the other. "It'll be okay, Kell. It'll be okay."

I want to believe her, but it's just not true. There's no way I'll be able to work for a while, and it'll be impossible to catch up in time. "No, Mer. It won't. There's too much... I have so much to do, plus work, and I need a shower, and then the rain plan and Tyler said–" and I break down again.

"Okay," she says with the patience of a saint. "Let's get you back to bed, huh?" She helps me up and walks me to my room, where I sit down on the side of my bed and start crying again.

A moment later, Merren hands me a clean shirt and tells me to change while she gets me a rag and a bucket. I pull my dirty, sweaty tank top over my head, pausing to release a fresh sob in the middle of the process, then put on the clean shirt and lie back with my head on the pillow. The room starts to wobble, and I close my eyes.

When Merren returns, she pulls the blanket over me and lays a cool, wet washcloth on my head. "I'm putting this bucket right here in case you need it, okay?" I nod and take a shaky breath as my lip quivers pathetically. "There, there," she says, tucking me in like my mom used to when I was a kid. "I put your phone on the charger. It was dead but has a little juice already. I'm going to clean up the bathroom and take a load of laundry over to housekeeping before my shift, and I'll let your mom know you're sick and can't work today–"

"But the festival, Mer. I have so much…" My words fade into a soft cry.

"Honey, it's alright. You'll catch up–"

"No! I won't be able to. Don't you see? Phase two starts today, and I have to–"

"Rest and feel better. That's what you have to do, Kell. Besides, Vinny can take care of things," she says and I fucking lose it. My soft cry escalates to a raging downpour at the thought of the festival and my promotion riding on Vinny. I might as well throw in the towel right now.

"Come on, Kell. It's not that bad. You'll be better soon, just try to get some rest and don't think about it. I'll check on you in a little while. Let me know if you need anything." Merren leaves the room, and I lie in the dark, tears streaming down my cheeks as the room and everything in my life spin out of control.

* * *

I wake up and have no idea if it's been three minutes or three years since Merren was here. I slide my phone off the nightstand and check the time. It's almost nine, and Tyler sent me a message.

Looks like we all got food poisoning. Hope you're ok.

I am not fucking okay. I drop the phone back on my nightstand and roll onto my side. Mistake! Mistake! Big ass mistake. My nausea goes from an EF3 to an EF5 immediately, and I reach for the bucket. How is there anything left inside me? I feel like even my soul has been expunged from my body.

With my sick bucket in hand, I shuffle to the bathroom and dump it out before washing my hands and rinsing my mouth. Then, I return to my bed and try to escape this hellish reality.

I doze off into a light sleep for just a few minutes but stir when I hear the apartment door open. It's probably Mer coming to check on me— or one of my parents. There's shuffling and indiscernible noises, then I hear a soft knock on my door and open my eyes to see Vinny. *Fuckin' Vinny.* In my apartment. In my room. Holding my festival binder!

"What are you doing here?" I ask and hate the way I sound so damn weak right now.

"Came by to get this," he says, motioning to *my* binder. "Phase two, right?"

I shake my head and push myself up to sit against the headboard. "No– No, you can't. It'll be a fucking disaster. Give that back," I say, reaching for the binder.

"Trade," he says and tosses me a bottle of pills. I miss the catch and he smirks. Fucking asshole, I'm sick and I wasn't even ready for it.

"I'm not taking drugs from you. I already feel like death warmed over."

"Mmm, tasty," he says and sits down on the side of my bed, placing my binder on the other side of him and out of my reach. "Those are from your mom. See?"

83

I look at the prescription bottle: *Melanie Daniels, take every eight hours as needed for nausea and vomiting.* Oh, fucking hell. I open the bottle and place a tiny pill in my mouth to dissolve.

"Good girl," he says, patting my leg, and I swear if I had the strength right now, I'd slug him. "Need anything before I go?"

"Uh, yeah. I need my binder back. Everything's going to fall apart if I don't take care of it."

"Sorry, you're off the clock today–"

"No, there's too much riding on this. Nothing will get done if I don't take care of it."

"Oh, ye of little faith."

Reaching for the binder without success, I whine. "Give it to me, Vinny."

"If you only knew how many times I imagined you saying that…"

He's teasing me. Fucker. I've never felt worse in my life and he's sitting here teasing me when I'm too damn weak to fight back. But the way he looks at me—like he might just go for it here and now on my sickbed—it *should* make me want to hurl, but it doesn't. For the first time today, the flutter in my stomach has nothing to do with the bad food I ate last night.

He leans closer to me, and I'm suddenly aware of how putrid I must smell. Lovely. "Since I can't give you what you really want," he says, brushing his hand along my bedhead. "Is there anything else I can do before I go?"

Fuck. This isn't good. My body's central command is overloaded with every mixed single in the book. *Yes. No. Fuck him. Don't. Kiss him. Cry.* I can't find my way to clarity, so I shake my head and resist the impulse to throw myself into his arms.

Vinny starts to stand up, and I reach for his hand. "Can you just let me know when you finish the first half of Phase Two?"

"Is that your way of asking me to stop by and check on you later?"

"Wha–" He takes the binder and pulls out a sheet, holding it up for me to see. It's my Phase Two checklist for today, and at the bottom, he added *Check on Kell.*

I could cry. I hate that I get so emotional when I'm sick, but what the hell kind of move is that? "Why are you being so nice to me?" I ask him.

"I'm not," he says with a shrug and returns the paper to the binder. I raise an eyebrow, calling him on it. He pulls a face and feigns disgust. "You look like shit. See?"

"Fuck you!"

"There she is," he says and looks at me in that way again—the way that hits my impulse control like a fucking nuke of desire. He needs to get up and walk out that door right now before this becomes the most confusing and sexually gratifying sick day of my life. Vinny leans over and kisses my forehead. Dammit, I want to kiss him right now, but I still feel like shit, and I know I look like shit—probably taste like shit too. He saves me from my indecision and stands up, binder in hand. "Don't worry, no one knows. I'm still your dirty little secret."

"All-American Rejects?" I ask. "That's the best you got?"

LOVER BOY BLUES

Tuesday, May 26, 2009: Vinny

After I left Kellyn's, I helped Mr. Cole with lawn work and replaced the lock on one of the cabins that was busted by some rowdy guests. Then I made my rounds, checking for repairs and picking up trash before lugging Kellyn's encyclopedia-length binder up to my room.

It takes me a good half hour to familiarize myself with her note system, including the color-coordinated tabs, cross-references, and *footnotes?!* I shake my head as I peruse the contents—this woman could take over the world with her organizational skills. When I finally feel acclimated enough to not fuck everything up, I start chipping away at the day's tasks. I call and confirm that we're on the schedule for extra trash bins and pick up the day of the event. The paramedics are good to go. The tents will be delivered and set up the day before the festival and the portable fences too.

I make a few notes *on a Post-it* and stick it to the inside of the binder so I don't mar Kellyn's carefully created and aesthetically pleasing project. Then I check with Mr. Cole to see if he has any pressing tasks for me, but everything's steady at the moment. It's almost six, so Kellyn will be due for another pill soon if she needs it. I hop in the golf cart and drive over to her apartment and let myself in. We never lock our doors during the summer season—there's no point.

"Housekeeping," I say, as I step into the living room and place Kellyn's binder on the coffee table. Merren must not be back yet because everything is quiet and the lights are still off. I peek inside Kellyn's room—she's asleep, and she has a washcloth in her hand. I grab a little white rag from the hall linen closet and walk into the bathroom, where I run it under the faucet, adjusting the water to a comfortable temperature before ringing out the excess.

Back in Kellyn's bedroom, I fold the rag into a long rectangle and gently lay it on her forehead. She stirs a little, and as I take the old one from her hand, she opens her eyes. "How are you feeling?" I ask.

She blinks in confusion, her deep blue eyes somehow darker now. "Better, I think."

I pull the folded-up list from my pocket and hand it to her. Every box is checked. She chuckles weakly as she runs her finger down the bulleted list. "Thank you," she says.

This may be the first time I've ever heard Kellyn genuinely thank me. Part of me wants to razz her about it, but a bigger part of me wants to pull her into my arms and kiss her, make her forget all about Tyler and the festival and her sickness and the whole world. But as each day goes by, my feelings become stronger, and there's too much on the line to take that chance again. When Tabitha blew everything up, including my heart, it sucked balls. But *this*—this would take me out for good. Tabitha never got under my skin. She never weaseled her way into my head. She never burrowed her clutches into my heart like Kellyn has.

I sit down on the side of her bed. "You're welcome, and…you don't look like shit," I say, taking her water-pruned hand in mine, turning it over, and running my thumb across her raisin-like fingers. "You never look like shit."

She closes her hand over mine, and my heart lodges itself in my throat. "Your fingers look like you've been swimming all day," I say because I really don't know which way to go right now.

"Or swimming all *night*?" she asks, looking down at our hands, then shifting her eyes to mine with a challenge. How the fuck did she find out about that?

"Wha–"

"After hours, and with guests… That's against the rules, you know," she says, her eyes back down on our hands.

"Didn't seem to care about the rules when it was you and me last summer."

When Kellyn looks up at me, I see in her eyes everything I feel—desire, regret, fear, longing. The problem is, even if we both want the same thing, we're too different and we're both afraid of what this would cost us. We're like the perfect match made in hell.

"Hey, Kell, I'm home," Merren calls out from the other room.

"Get some rest," I tell her and pull her wrinkled fingers to my lips, where I kiss them softly and let them go just as Merren walks into the room.

* * *

Wednesday, May 27, 2009

Kellyn must be feeling better because I saw her zipping around the resort in her golf cart this morning. She hasn't tracked me down to work on the festival planning or gripe me out for wearing the wrong shirt, and it's actually turning out to be a suckass day because of it.

I spent the first half of the workday helping Mr. Cole, and now I'm finishing up my shift at the grill with Morgan and JT. It's not too busy tonight since Wednesday is Luau night at the main house and *everyone* wants to get lei'd.

"Vinny, my man," JT says, bundling up his grease-stained apron and tossing it at me. I catch it midair and chuck it in the hamper by the wall. "You missed out the other night. Tsk, tsk, tsk." He shakes his head in exaggerated disappointment.

"Think I'll live," I tell him, picking up a stray onion that never made it into the basket and tossing it from one hand to the other.

Morgan takes a seat on the counter and looks from JT to me. "What's he talking about?"

JT stares me down with a mischievous grin, but I just roll my eyes and keep tossing the onion. Whatever he thinks he's got on me, it's nothing Morgan doesn't already suspect.

"Our buddy here came down with the lover boy blues Monday night. Had to call in sick and left me working a double feature."

"Uh-oh," Morgan says, eyes wide and shaking her head. "She got to ya, huh? I knew it!"

I place the onion in the basket where it belongs and check the time —still half an hour to go with these two. "I have no idea what you're talking about. Y'all get into Teak's weed again?"

"Ha! I wish," Morgan says. "I knew there was something going on between you guys."

"There's nothing–"

"Then explain Monday night," JT says and hops up on the counter beside Morgan.

Leaning back against the sink, I cross my arms and tell him again. "It was stress, dude. I told you. I was tired and stressed. That's it."

As JT and Morgan discuss the validity of my claims, I pull out my cell to check for a message from Kellyn, but I know I won't find anything. I hope she's just busy, trying to catch up on yesterday's work and not avoiding me. But even if she is, she won't avoid her responsibilities, so I bet on that and type out a message, letting her know I confirmed the extra equipment deliveries for the festival.

Less than a minute after I push send, she replies: *Great. Security staff and shuttle service confirmed today. Just need to contact parking attendants.*

It's work-related and devoid of emotion, but it's contact. It's a starting point.

LITTLE MISS OBEDIENT BROKE A RULE

Thursday, May 28, 2009: Kellyn

"Glad to see you eating something other than crackers and jello," Merren says, joining me at the little dining table in the employee break room.

I swallow my mouthful of macaroni and cheese with a nod. "I knew I'd need to carb load for changeover. I can't even count how many late checks I handled this morning."

"Tonight can't come soon enough," she says with a deep sigh. "How's Tyler? Feeling better?"

I lay down my spoon and blow out an exasperated breath. This whole Tyler-Vinny thing is messing with my head. "Yeah, think so." My shrug and most likely my face catch Merren's attention.

"What is it? I thought you had a good date, aside from the food poisoning after."

"It was...okay," I say, at a loss for how to categorize it. "But then, towards the end, the chemistry disappeared, and I was actually repulsed by his touch. I thought it was just him, you know? But maybe it wasn't. Maybe it was the food poisoning." I slide the macaroni out of the way and slump forward, laying my head on the table as I groan.

"Okay, I'm confused. What's happening here? Do you still like him or not?"

"I don't know," I whine and then sit back up. "I don't know! I *want* to like him. I did everything I could to feel something when we kissed, but… Ugh, I don't know, maybe the food we ate fucked up the chemistry. Think I should test the theory? You know, meet up with him and try it again now that we're both feeling better?"

Merren's sweet, motherly smile tells me the advice she's about to offer may not be well received. "Kell, if you have to think about it or test a theory, I don't think there's anything there." She reaches across the table and holds my hand. "I think that if you really liked him, you'd still feel something even when you're puking your guts out. I don't think that kind of thing goes away when you're at your worst… If anything, I think it grows."

Fuck. If I didn't know Merren like I do, I'd wonder if she spied on my visits with Vinny when I was sick. I'd wonder if she somehow got inside my brain and heart for a front-row seat to this whole disaster of a love story.

Merren shrugs and releases my hand as she stands up from the table. "Just my opinion though… You know your heart better than I do, Kell."

Three short honks tell us Kade is outside waiting for us to ride down to the lake with him. I grab the bag of s'more ingredients off the counter and follow Merren out to the truck. "Ice chest in the back?" I ask Kade as I climb inside the cab and pull the door shut.

"Yeah, just filled it up. Picked up some Smirnoff Ice for you, too," Kade says.

"What–why? I don't even like those." Scrunching up my face in disgust, I turn to look at him. His cheeks are red, and out of my peripheral vision, I see Merren biting her lip as if to keep herself from saying something.

"Uhh… You don't?" Kade asks nervously.

"*I* asked for them," Merren says quickly. "God, your memory is starting to go, old man." She nudges me and tries to laugh it off with an eye roll for emphasis. I swear, those two are the worst liars on the planet. It's so obvious there's something going on between them. If I weren't at full capacity dealing with my own drama, I'd be pissed at her for keeping it from me.

When we get down to the lake, Kade unloads the ice chest while Merren and I carry camper chairs to the fire pit. Heidi, Morgan, and Dane come flying up behind us in a golf cart, and not long after, JT, Vinny, and Teak arrive in theirs.

While Morgan and Dane play around, kissing and flirting like the perfect couple, Heidi hollers at JT, tossing a football in his direction. "Wanna start a fire?"

He catches it and carelessly flings it back over his shoulder to Teak, who fumbles. "With you, girl?" JT says, raising his eyebrows. "Always."

Heidi isn't fazed by JT's antics and rolls her eyes as she walks across the uneven terrain like a Victoria's Secret model on location. They've hooked up a time or twelve, but Heidi has this confidence about her that seems to make it so easy for her to just do whatever the hell she wants to in life. I don't understand how she does it, but she doesn't let things become awkward between them—or anyone she's taken a turn with, for that matter. Hell, she even hooked up with Kade back in high school, and here they are, totally chill, working together—friends even.

Then there's me. And fuckin' Vinny. I was spinning out last summer—stressed about going away to college, freaking out about making new friends and finding time to work and study, and already missing home before I even left. I was overwhelmed, and life felt suddenly out of control. Then along came Vinny with his infuriating sarcasm and fuck-if-I-care attitude, refusing to patronize me.

It was a perfect battle of wits—no matter what I said to defend my self-perceived crisis, he had a comeback that put me in my place. In some fucked up way, arguing with Vinny was therapeutic. It siphoned all of my worry and stress about college into the tension building between us, and when it came to a head, the explosion that followed was hot and exciting and everything I needed.

I thought the one time would be enough to settle my nerves—to get it all out of my system. But I messed up and went back for more the next day. And then a third time. Thank God, I had to pack up and leave for school that week, or who knows what would have happened. I was becoming addicted, and quitting Vinny cold turkey was the only way out.

Now, here I am, playing the same game with him this summer, only the stakes are higher because now I know what it is I could lose. And dammit, I don't want to lose what I had with him.

"S'more?" Merren asks, interrupting my thoughts as she holds out the bag of marshmallows.

"Yeah, sure," I say, taking one and picking up a skewer to impale the pure white pillow of sugar. We walk over to the fire pit, where JT and Heidi have already claimed their spots. I squat down near the fire and stick the marshmallow into the flames, watching it scorch and bubble up under the heat. The others join us, passing around drinks and marshmallows and skewers.

"Damn, Kellyn, why don't you just eat the ash?" JT says when I pull my blackened marshmallow from the fire and blow out the flame. I sit down beside Merren and assemble my s'more. On the other side of me, Morgan sits on Dane's lap, feeding him a marshmallow. Dark is settling fast now, and it's becoming hard to see past the light of the flames, but I steal a glance at Vinny, sitting on the other side, tapping his fingers on the neck of his beer bottle and staring into the fire.

I sit back in the camper chair and close my eyes. A cool breeze floats in off the lake, lifting the tiny hairs on my arm. Soft conversations and occasional outbursts of laughter interrupt the fire's rolling crackles and pops. *This* is why we come down here every Thursday night. *This* is our time.

"Okay, who's starting it tonight?" Heidi asks.

"I got it," Kade says, and I open my eyes to see him standing up with his drink raised high. "Never have I ever shown up to work with a hangover."

Teak throws his hands up in the air. "Seriously? How is that possible?"

"Oh, you know…" JT says and takes a drink. "Mr. Responsible."

Kade takes a flourished bow before sitting down on the other side of Merren and telling her she's up next. "Hmm," she says, strumming her fingers on her knees. "Never have I ever… Oh! Never have I ever lost my underwear in the lake." Laughter and accusations explode into the night, and not one, but *two* guilty parties come forward—Morgan and JT. I can't say I'm all that surprised about JT.

"You're up, Kell," Merren says, and I look around the fire, trying to recall the group's collection of sins and misdemeanors.

"Alright," I say. "Never have I ever dated my ex."

"Well, that feels like a targeted attack," Morgan says with a laugh before slinging back her drink in unison with Dane.

I lean over my knees to see if Kade's following the rules. "You too, bro." He shoots me a sarcastic smile and takes a drink.

When I sit back in my chair, I notice JT whispering something to Morgan and Dane—colluding to take someone down, most likely. "My turn," Morgan says, holding her drink out, pinky up and back straight as she perches on Dane's lap. "Never have I ever hooked up in the resort hot tub."

My stomach drops, and I feel the heat of the campfire on my face. Teasing whispers of speculation echo around the circle as I stare into my drink. I can feel someone looking at me, and I know just who it is. Fuck it. I take a sip, and the group goes wild. In the commotion, I look up at Vinny, whose eyes have been on me the whole time. He takes a drink, and another round of shouting and laughter erupts, feeding the flame that hadn't fully died down to begin with.

Merren turns to me, her face full of bewildered laughter. "Holy shit, Kell! I have no words…"

"Little Miss Obedient broke a rule? I'll drink to that," Dane shouts.

"Nah, I don't believe it," Heidi says, shaking her head with a hint of a stink eye. There's always been a touch of animosity between us, but that's an ancient story for another time. "I mean, Vinny," Heidi says, holding her beer bottle out toward him. "Sure, *that* I believe, but not Kellyn."

"Oh, believe it, baby, I saw it with my own two eyes," JT says, clearly feeling his buzz already. This reveal shocks everyone, including me because what the actual fuck, JT? Now everyone's scrambling to guess who I was with and begging JT for clues or an outright answer. Even Merren takes a guess, but no one's even close. It's so obvious and right in front of them—but they're too buzzed to catch on.

Since the game has spiraled into a chaotic round of Guess Who, I stand up and take my drink down to the shore to get some air. Meanwhile, the group's laughter, excited guesses, and obscure conversation drift into the night. I take a sip of my drink and look out across the dark water, but when someone tugs on my ponytail, I snap my head back to see who it is.

"You know, I learned something about you the other day," Vinny says as he sits down beside me, and I'm taken aback by how fucking happy I am that he's here. Since everything started with him last summer, I've felt a lot of things—irritation, confusion, passion. But happiness? This is new.

"You're a slob," he says, nudging me.

"Wha– I am not!"

He looks over his shoulder at me, dropping his head just so. "Your room was worse than JT's."

"I was sick. It's not usually like that. You can ask Merren."

"Suuuure," he says, looking out at the lake.

I scoff at the hypocrisy. "Sorry my sickbed wasn't up to your ironically high standards."

"I'm teasing you, you know?" He turns to meet my eyes in the moonlight. "I just like to push your buttons. Get you all fired up. Thought you'd have figured that out by now."

"Why? What's in it for you?" I ask. He leans back on his arms, shaking his head. "What?" I shrug.

"Are you honestly asking me?" His tone is like it was when I was sick and he came to check on me—when he held my hand and kissed my fingers. I try to read his eyes, but it's too dark away from the firelight.

"You're so put together and perfect all the time," he says. "All business and order… But there's something about you when the chaos breaks through and wakes you up. You're like a firework when the fuse runs out. It's fucking beautiful, Kellyn. It turns me on."

My heart is so full right now that it's hard to get my breath. This is what I wanted to feel the other night on the boat. *This* is what I couldn't make myself feel for Tyler. How the fuck is Vinny making me feel this way without even touching me?

"What are y'all doing over there?" Morgan hollers at us, and someone else catcalls.

"I'll go," Vinny says, standing up. "Don't worry, I'll say we were talking about the festival."

I'm still trying to process the way I feel at this moment, and I can't switch gears fast enough to tell him to stay. All I can do as I look up at him and his beautiful face shadowed in the moonlight is nod. I'm frozen and confused and scared because I think I'm falling for fuckin' Vinny.

He returns to the group, leaving me by the shore, and it's lonely now—something is missing, like the day Granny Kay brought me down here and told me about the water spirits and the promise that they would guide me if ever I needed them. Fuck, I've never needed them more. I scoot closer to dip my fingers into the water and send out a silent prayer to whatever magic lives in Sweetwater Lake.

THAT'S THE PLAN, BOSS

Thursday, May 28, 2009: Vinny

"What was that all about?" JT asks when I rejoin the group around the fire.

"Work stuff," I say, avoiding his eyes.

"Bullshit."

"I'm serious. She's stressed about the festival. We still have a shit ton to do." I run my hands over my face and groan. "Fuck, I'm tired, man. Think I'm gonna cut out early. You and Teak catch a ride with the others?"

"Sure, no problem. Oh, quick question, I have a date later, will you and Kellyn be using the hot tub tonight?" he asks in a hushed voice but bursts out laughing immediately after.

"Fuck off, JT," I say and clap him on the back before heading out.

There's a hint of rain in the air as I drive back to the apartment. I vaguely remember the forecast mentioning a chance, but it didn't look promising. Still, I park the golf cart on the porch where the awning will offer a little coverage at least.

I didn't want to leave the party. I would have stayed there all night, sitting with Kellyn by the water, but it was too risky after JT's shenanigans. I could have beat his ass for telling Morgan about the hot tub. I don't know exactly what he said, but after tonight, it's only a matter of time before someone puts it together or pulls it out of JT, and when that happens, Kellyn's gonna be fucking pissed. It's the beginning of the end, and I'd rather not stick around for the fallout.

The living room is messier than usual, and I search high and low for the remote, flipping cushions and sliding furniture around, but I still can't find it. I was just trying to distract myself, dammit. Dropping to the couch, I run my hands through my hair. I'm about three seconds away from pulling it out when the door opens, and I see Kellyn standing in my apartment. I sit up immediately and try to read her expression. She's usually so transparent, but right now, I can't even pick up a hint. "You okay? Why'd you guys come back early?" I ask and meet her by the door.

"It's just me. I caught a ride back with Morgan. She and Dane got into it again," she says, rolling her eyes and shifting her weight from one leg to the other and then back. She's nervous. That's something.

"Oh…umm. What are–"

"What happened Monday night?" She brushes past me and walks toward the kitchen.

"Monday night?" I repeat, turning to follow her. "Let's see… You went out with Mr. Perfect, who then poisoned you–"

"No," she says, turning around abruptly, hands on her sexy little hips. "At the pool."

I can't tell if she's jealous or just here to rake me over the coals for breaking the damn rules again. "Nothing happened."

She crosses her arms, closing her eyes as she takes in a long, deep breath, and when she opens them again, they're sparking up. "I saw you, Vinny."

"Oh yeah? What did you see?" I lock my eyes on hers, a challenge to show her cards. I need to know this isn't just about breaking the fucking rules. I need to know that it bothered her to think of me with someone else.

"You and a whole herd of female guests going into the pool after hours," she says, bringing her pouty little mouth to a point when she finishes.

I take a step closer, flicking my lip ring as I do, just to see if it affects her. She responds exactly as I hoped, with little specks of red gathering on her cheeks. "And what part of that bothered you, huh?"

Her lips part for words she can't find, and I take another step, close enough that she has to tilt her pretty little head back to look me in the eyes.

"Tell me, Kellyn, was it that *I* went into the pool after hours?" Her breathing picks up, and I take the loose strand of sun-kissed hair that brushes her cheek between my index and thumb, slowly sliding my fingers down its length, memorizing the buttery smooth texture. When I get to the end, I let it drop and shake my head.

"Or was it that I took guests into the pool *after hours*?" She blinks quickly, like she's trying to shield her eyes from the sun, and starts to speak, but I place my thumb over her bottom lip, watching it follow as I give it the slightest tug.

"Or maybe..." I pause to appreciate how fucking beautiful she is as she stares up at me, her deep blue eyes swimming with anticipation, her cheeks flushed, and her mouth soft with lips parted just waiting for me to take them. This energy between us is strong enough to set the world on fire with one spark, and I swallow hard. What's about to happen is undeniable.

"Or maybe it was that I took *female guests* into the pool after hours," I say, and light the powder keg. All at once, her hands are crawling up my chest as I lift her into my arms and we fight each other for control of the kiss, but when her soft little whimper enters my mouth, I pull her body tighter against mine and carry her through the apartment and up the stairs to my room.

By the time we reach the landing, her hands are tugging on my hair as she squeezes her legs around my waist. Fuck me, this feels good. I stumble but recover, bracing the wall with one hand for support, and the commotion that follows as we slam against it brings laughter to her lips. I rest my forehead against hers as we catch our breath, and she slowly lowers herself to stand, back against the wall.

She trails her hands from the back of my neck around to my chest and down to the hem of my tee shirt. When she raises her heavy-lidded eyes to mine, I watch them flicker to life a split second before she pulls my shirt, bringing me an inch closer to her. "Your room isn't clean either!"

I steal a kiss before lifting my shirt over my head. "Never said it would be." I pick her up again as she continues her analysis.

"But the last time I was here–"

"Yeah, I cleaned it because I thought you might come by," I say and kiss her again.

She pulls away. "What?"

I try for another, but she dodges me, requiring an answer to cross the bridge. I kiss her cheek instead. "I asked JT to cover for me"—I move my mouth down to her neck and kiss her salty, sweet skin—"so I could run back here and clean up. He thought I had a date." I chuckle and return to claim my passage, and when she kisses me, arching her back, I move toward the bed.

She pulls away again. "Wait–why? Why did you–"

I take advantage of the opportunity to catch my breath before I answer. We're almost to the place where she lets go of everything and gives up her possessive little grip on control, but we're not there yet, so I'll play along and answer any question she has, knowing we're getting closer and closer with each one.

"I didn't think it would impress you if that's what you're wondering." I give her ass a little lift as I shift her weight in my arms for a better hold. "Thought it might get under your skin," I say and nip at her neck before pulling back to look her in the eyes. "You always think you have me pegged." I steal a quick kiss. "You get so hot and flustered when you're wrong. It's sexy as hell." I drop to my knees, landing on the bed and laying her down with a gentle tumble.

"You're such an asshole, Vinny," she says and kisses me again.

"I know"—kiss—"and you love it."

"Fuck you."

"That's the plan, Boss," I say, sitting back on my knees and unbuttoning her shorts. She wiggles them down her legs, and I toss them aside. Then I kick off my jeans as she lifts her tee shirt over her head.

"God, you're beautiful, Kell," I say and lean down to kiss her stomach, then her sternum and the top of her breast, her shoulder, her neck. She wraps her legs around me and manages to slip her feet under the elastic of my boxers, working them off my ass as I plant kisses all over her skin. She smells like summer nights, sweet with a touch of salt and earth riding on the clouds of toasted wood.

"Switch places with me," she says, and I roll onto my back. When I reach down to give myself a little relief, she smacks my hand away and crawls on top of me.

"Not fair," I say, pushing against her and grabbing her thighs to hold her in place. "You still have clothes on."

Tilting her head to the side, she slowly reaches her arms behind her back and unhooks her bra, releasing her perky little breasts with a teasing grin. "Better?"

I shrug then nod my head down toward her panties. She bends forward on her knees, her hands pressed against the wall behind my head and her breasts hovering over my chest as the hard little nubs tease me with every graze. "Well," she says, dropping her eyes to my mouth. "What are you gonna do about it?"

I waste no time and slide my hands up and over her ass, hooking my fingers under her thong and working it down to her thighs. She keeps her hands on the wall for support as she kicks it off, and just as she's about to sit back down, I take her ass cheeks in my hands and pull her up my body, positioning her within reach of my mouth.

"Vinny–" she starts but gives it up as soon as the breath from my *shhh* hits her sweet little clit. As I kiss her lips and taste her excitement on my tongue, she rewards me with moans and sexy little whimpers that almost take me out, but I resist, holding out for the moment I can watch her lose herself *with* me. She's getting closer, rocking on my face with a rhythm that picks up speed every few seconds. I lap my tongue against her, taking everything I can like I may never taste it again as I knead her perfectly round ass with my hands. Her approval becomes louder with each breath, and when she slams her hands against the wall, I know it's time. I start at the bottom and slowly run my tongue all the way to the top, where I angle my mouth to suck that sweet little pearl of hers as she cries out. And when her legs begin to tremble, I drag my bottom lip along the same slow, agonizing path, tantalizing her needy flesh with the cool metal hanging from my lip.

Her mountain crumbles around me, and I gather her into my arms, moving over so she can lie beside me. While she settles like falling snow, I reach across to the side of my bed and grab a condom. Propped up on one elbow, I look down at her and run my free hand along the curvature of her face. She turns into my palm, placing a kiss there before blinking her eyes open.

"Come here," she says, hooking her index finger. I bring my mouth to hers with the intention of kissing her softly, but she pulls me tight against her lips and opens to take my tongue. When she moans into my mouth, I pull away, breaking the kiss with a raspy breath.

"Kell, I–"

"I'm ready," she says.

I hand her the condom as I position myself above her, and she reaches down between us to roll it over my length. It's almost enough to end me, but I clench my jaw and gain control. As soon as it's in place, Kellyn raises her hips toward me and runs her hands along my arms and shoulders. With one arm supporting my weight, I take her leg and bend it toward her, then move slowly, savoring every inch of her I can claim. God, her face—her mouth parts as breath comes harder and faster, and her eyes flicker open then roll back and close again. I don't think she has any idea what she's doing to me. She's consumed by this moment—the way she feels. And fuck, I'm almost there too.

Kellyn's sighs and soft moans grow louder, and I join her. It just feeds her arousal, which, in turn, feeds mine. With each movement, we inch closer to the mountaintop, but when we hear the front door open and voices downstairs, we freeze. Her eyes are wide, but a smile tickles the side of her mouth, and something about that smile on her face while I'm inside of her stokes the fire already blazing through me. I can't help it, I *have* to continue. She seems to agree with my decision, but soon she's fighting herself for control, biting her lip, clapping her hand over her mouth, and smacking the mattress with her palm.

I know she's frustrated—I can see it on her face and feel it in her body. She wants more—*needs* more. And fuck, I do too. I try slowing it down, thinking that might satisfy her without the noise, but it feels too damn good, and she's fighting herself again.

"Yo, Vinny!" Teak shouts from the bottom of the stairs. We both freeze, staring into each other's eyes as we wait. Then JT's voice joins in, calling for me. I know it's not the best time, but my God, I need to move. I don't know if it's because we're frozen still, muscles locked in place, or something else, but the hold this woman has on me right now is impossible to ignore—even for a second. I back out slowly, and her eyes shoot to mine, full of pleading. I place a hand over hers, linking our fingers, and pull as far out as I can without losing touch, then slowly return, pushing as deep into her as I can. Her sigh is hardly audible, but her face relaxes in response to my movements. I go again, and this time it's me—a soft growl-like moan escapes, and I don't even regret it because this feels so damn good.

Kellyn covers my mouth with her hand, but it doesn't stop the next moan from coming out, and louder, the vibration tickling her palm. When she laughs, her eyes shoot wide, and I let go of her hand so I can cover her mouth. This may work—we manage to muffle our praise as I continue to work slow, deep thrusts in and out, in and out. I'm handling it just fine, but I can tell she's battling for control again. I'm not doing this without her, and

I'm not going to let her hold herself back. We both need this, and we need it completely.

I shift my body to find a deeper angle and go again. The look on her face when she takes it tells me this is it—she's not going to win this war for control. I slide out and rock back in, putting all of myself into reaching her as deeply as I can, and she gasps against my hand. I nod. "Yeah, Boss, we're doing this," I whisper. She removes her hand from my mouth and pulls at her hair as I go again, and again. She's still fighting it.

"Just let go. It'll be okay," I tell her and kiss her forehead before pulling back out and going again. This time, I'm not letting up, and she knows it. As I pick up speed and she opens herself up to me, she whimpers and moans into my hand. At one point, she nips at it, then pulls back with a look of worry in her eyes. "It's alright," I tell her. "Whatever you gotta do is fine."

She nods, eyes wide and exhaling slowly. No holding back now. I start again, going deep and then sliding out all the way to the tip, bringing us both to the point of begging before rocking back inside her as deep as I can, never wanting to leave, but needing the friction. She writhes under me, hiking her knees up to her chest and arching her back to give me every possible inch of her body. The next thrust brings a small moan from her, muffled by my flesh against her mouth, but when I pull back to the edge of all hell breaking loose and push back into her with greater force than before, she clamps down on my hand.

Fuck, it hurts so bad, but everything else feels so damn good. The scales tip in the favor of passion, and I go again. Then again, and again, and each time the crescendo builds, her bite digs a little deeper as her cry grows louder. We're toast. I don't even fucking care anymore. We'll deal with the fallout tomorrow. I'm one step away from the mountaintop, and I'm taking the leap. And just as I do, Kellyn constricts around me, squeezing tighter than I've ever felt, and I give her everything I have. I'm spent, and sweaty, and satisfied, and my hand hurts like a mother fucker, but the look on Kellyn's face is worth it.

This girl... In my bed, all tangled up in my arms, lighter than a feather and floating higher than Snoop ever could... This girl has fucking ruined me, and I love it.

YOUR FACE IS AN OPEN BOOK

Thursday, May 28, 2009: Kellyn

Holy shit. That was better than I remember, and the way I feel right now in Vinny's arms is like a perfect high, warm and light, safe and content. I snuggle against him, bringing his hand to my lips when he winces.

"What's wrong?" I pull back to see his face and follow his eyes down to his hand in mine, where I find a deep pink stamp of teeth marks. "Shit, Vinny! Why did you let me do that? Didn't it hurt?"

He scoffs. "Yeah, it hurt. Hurt like hell, but I was busting through the gates of heaven, Kell. I wasn't about to stop you."

And just like that, somehow I reach a new high—I didn't think it was possible, and certainly not with mere words. He kisses my head as I lay it back down on his chest and close my eyes, and we fall asleep to the cicada song playing outside his window.

Friday, May 29, 2009

"Are you gonna come clean?" Merren asks, scooping popcorn into a red and white striped paper bag that she then hands to a little girl with pigtails.

I make change for a twenty and hand it to the girl's mother with a smile. "I'm sorry?" I say out of the corner of my mouth.

"Come on," Merren says, pausing mid-scoop to look at me with an eyebrow hiked up. "Your dirty little secret." I freeze, waiting for her to divulge more before I craft a response.

"Where you were last night..." she says and dips her head. "I know you didn't get home until this morning. So were you with Tyler?" She resumes her popcorn duties and places the bag she just filled in the holder. "Or with Vinny?"

I choke on air or spit—or her words, most likely— and feel myself turning red in the cheeks. "I don't– What? Why would you say–"

"Well, you both left early... Then there's the fact that he drives you crazy."

"He does not..." I try my hand at lying, and her face tells me I failed. Pshh. Like she has any room to talk.

"Oh, Kell," she says, pulling me into a side hug. "Babe, your face is an open book, and I'm an avid reader."

I'm torn because, after last night, I want to gush to my best friend about this wonderful guy who makes the world explode into a kaleidoscope of color when he touches me. This guy who can infuriate me and turn me on in the same instant. This guy who I can't stop thinking about or looking for at every turn. But it's Vinny...and he's impossible. He doesn't give a fuck about rules or responsibilities. He doesn't even seem to have a plan for his life beyond working the grill and maintenance—at least I'm aiming for growth at Sweetwater. We're too different, and the effect he has on me is dangerous. I'm afraid his chaos will change me—make me more like him.

The concession orders finally slow down as Lightning McQueen makes it into Radiator Springs. Talking cars illuminate the little movie screen as families and kids sit in wonder, making memories they'll keep with them long after they leave this place.

I wipe down the counter and tidy the candy display while Merren reads something on her phone screen. With a quiet chuckle, her mouth curls into a swoony smile, and I would bet money she's texting Kade. Part of me wants to ask her if she's ready to spill her dirty little secret, but the other part of me doesn't want to risk hearing those details about my brother.

With nothing left to clean at the moment, I hop on one of the bar stools that sits along the back counter and watch the movie for the millionth time, tapping my toes to the catchy tunes and even laughing out loud at Mater's classic lines.

When the credits start rolling, I stand up, stretching and gathering the energy to clean the rest of the cinema once the crowd funnels out. It doesn't take too long since Mer and I already cleaned the concession stand and the guests were fairly neat tonight. By half past seven, we lock up and take the golf cart over to the grill for dinner. I park on the side of the building, and we walk around to the back entrance that leads to the kitchen.

Morgan is at the front counter, ringing up a guest, and JT is packing up an order. "What's up, my ladies?" he says when he spots us.

"Can I get a burger, pretty please?" Merren says sweetly, holding her hands together in prayer.

JT nods in my direction. "You too?"

"Sure," I say, looking around for Vinny but trying not to make it obvious. Merren washes her hands at the sink and says she'll drop the fries.

"Kell, will you grab another pack of buns from the pantry?" JT asks as he walks over to the grill.

"Sure," I say and walk back to the little hallway behind the kitchen. The pantry sits at the end of the hall. I hear shuffling as I approach, and when I step into the open doorway, I see Vinny taking inventory. I clear my throat, and he looks up from the clipboard he's holding.

"Hey, you," he says as the corner of his mouth hitches, and I notice his lip ring is in. "What did I do this time?"

I take a step into the pantry and point to his mouth. "What is it with you and rules?"

Vinny sets the clipboard aside and closes the space between us, pulling me against him with one hand on my waist. "What is it with you and my piercing?" he asks quietly, looking deep into my eyes and knowing full well what it is.

Warmth and need bloom behind my navel, and I grab two fistfuls of his green resort polo. "At least you're wearing the right color today," I say, my breath becoming heavier by the second.

"I'd rather be wearing you," he says and the world snaps out of focus. He's holding me tight against him and kissing me with fervor as my

116

grip on his shirt grows so tight it'll probably leave a stretch mark. He scoops my ass up into his arms and I wrap my legs around him as he kisses me deeper, his low grumbles and growls escaping into my mouth.

When he takes two steps toward the door, reaching out with one hand to push it shut, my knee hits a box of styrofoam containers, knocking it off the shelf. He presses my back against the wall for support, and I hold his head in my hands, working my fingers up the back of his neck and raking them through his dark tousled hair.

"Kell, what's the holdup? I need those buns," JT hollers from the hall, his voice growing louder as he approaches the pantry.

"I, umm…" My breathing is heavy and my heart is pounding. "Just a minute…"

Vinny lowers me to a standing position and tilts my chin upward with his index and thumb before he kisses me, soft and deep, full of tenderness and desire. And while the kiss is slow, it does nothing to steady my breathing or pounding heart—somehow it fans the flame and I'm fucked. In the best way.

"Come over tonight?" he whispers against my ear. "We'll say we're working on the festival."

I nod my head, and he kisses my temple before stepping away.

After dinner, I went home to shower and shave. Luckily, I didn't have to come up with an excuse for leaving because Mer said she had prep work to do at the activities center for the weekend. Likely story, but it works in my favor, so I let it slide.

I throw on some clean clothes and run across to Vinny's before he gets home. He and JT both work until nine, and Teak should be tending to the horses around this time, so I can sneak into their apartment unnoticed. When I step up to their door, I open it quietly, peeking inside—just in case. It's a wreck as usual, but no one's home.

I shoot upstairs, my heart needlessly pounding with adrenaline, but just knowing that I could be caught sends it racing. I kick off my sandals and sit down on his bed, taking deep, calming breaths. It looks like Vinny made an attempt at tidying up his room. The laundry is in one pile instead of scattered all over the floor—that's a start, and I wonder if he did it for me.

Checking the time on the alarm clock, I let out an exasperated groan. It's only eight-forty, so I still have time to kill. Across from the bed is a small TV, but it's probably best to keep it off in case anyone other than Vinny comes home and hears me up here. I look around for a quiet diversion instead, but the only book I can find is under his alarm clock and lamp, so I leave it undisturbed.

On the other side of the mattress is a collection of CDs. There's a lot of Green Day and Good Charlotte—mostly rock and punk albums, but I also find a few unexpected names like The La's and Bob Dylan. Then there's this Picasso-like cover, very abstract and eighties. The Outfield, it says. His collection is more varied than I expected. With nothing else to do, I organize the CDs in alphabetical order by artist, then by album name, then by color, and sit back to admire my aesthetically pleasing handiwork.

I check the clock again—eight fifty—and look around for something else to organize, but there's not much to work with. In the corner, I spot a black guitar case, which surprises me because I've never seen him play or even heard him talk about it. Seems like something he would have brought up in all of our planning for the festival. I can't imagine Vinny passing up the opportunity to put me in my place with his musical expertise.

I lay back on the bed and open my phone to clean out my message folder, but I did that last week, so it only takes a minute. Then I snap a picture of myself making kissy lips and send it to Vinny with the words *I'm ready*. Maybe it will speed up the process on his end.

Dropping my phone on the mattress with a sigh, I don't expect to receive a response, but when the notification dings, I scramble to read it.

Good. Don't leave. I'll be there asap.

How soon is that, I want to ask, but I don't want to come off as needy…except I'm feeling pretty damn needy right now. Just being here in his bed with the reminders of last night—it's turning me on, and my body longs for his touch. I can't lie still, so I stand up, pacing the floor and looking for a distraction. Aside from the CDs and television, which I've already ruled out, there's literally nothing to do in this room except fuck.

I flop down on the bed with a thud and stare at the ceiling for as long as I can, which is probably all of six seconds, before looking over to check the time again. Five till nine. I reach down and unbutton my shorts because every second counts, and I can't wait one second longer. Then I run some mental calculations and determine I can save at least ten more seconds if I lose my shorts and top altogether. So I slip out of them and crawl under the blanket.

Shit. I might have made things worse. My body knows what I came for, and now I'm lying here in his bed, stripped down to my underwear, begging time to hurry the fuck up. I flip onto my side and pull my knees up to my chest, trying to contain the desire humming under my skin. I swear, if Vinny doesn't get here soon, I might just fucking explode.

I text him again. *How much longer?*

And almost immediately, he replies: *Someone's impatient tonight. ;)*

Get your ass over here now.

On it, Boss.

I roll over with my back to the staircase landing and unhook my bra, then fling it away. It lands near the guitar case, and I pull the blanket tight over my body. Every little movement of the fabric piques the sensitive skin of my breasts. I roll my thumb over one nipple, feeling it harden in response to my touch, and I imagine it's Vinny's fingers, and mouth, and tongue, and *fuuuuck me.* I flip back over to the other side so I can check the time. Three minutes.

I let out a frustrated huff and trail my hands along my skin, stopping when my fingers run across the silky smooth fabric that's taking on heat and moisture as I squirm in desperation. *Fuckin' Vinny!* I rip the panties off and stretch out under the sheet, appreciating how damn good it feels to be completely bare and ready and turned on.

When I hear the door close downstairs and voices follow, I freeze in fear, but another wave of desire surges through me at the thought that Vinny might be here. I close my eyes and listen carefully, but I don't hear him—it's just Teak and JT. Are you fucking kidding me?

God, I need this. I don't want to start without him, but hell, I guess I already have. Spreading my hips wide and pulling my knees back, I reach down between my legs and stroke my fingers along the warm, sensitive skin, thinking of Vinny, and listening for him, but only hearing Teak and JT's obscured voices. Fuck, Vinny! I need you. *Right fucking now!*

And like an answered prayer, I hear the sound of the door again, and someone says his name. It's too much—knowing he's here—knowing that what I crave with everything in me is about to be delivered. I run my thumb over my clit, trying to appease it a while longer as I wait in writhing desperation for Vinny to come upstairs and fuck me.

Footsteps gather on the stairs, becoming louder as they approach. Then I hear JT's voice. If he fucks this up for me, I'll never forgive him. But as they reach the landing, Vinny peeks his head around the corner and spots me. Just seeing the look on his face amplifies everything I'm feeling, and I close my eyes, working my hand back and forth under the sheet.

He must say something to send JT away—I don't know—but when I open my eyes again, Vinny's standing above me, looking down with heady desire in his eyes. "Are you–are you naked under there, Kell?"

I can't speak, I just nod as a sigh escapes at the pleasure I'm giving myself and the sight of Vinny watching me. "Fuck… Kellyn, are you touching yourself?"

I nod and whimper as I do, wishing he would just get down here and put me out of my misery already. "Are you thinking about me?" he asks, kneeling beside the mattress, and I nod. His smile is so fucking sexy, and the way he's looking at me right now almost sends me over the edge.

"How long have you"—he lifts the sheet and peeks underneath —"Oh…" Dropping the sheet as his eyes find mine, he finally understands the measure of my need. He rips his clothes off faster than I could have imagined and crawls into bed with me, lifting the sheet and watching me. "Damn, it's hot watching you like this," he says, and I let out something between a whine and a groan. His eyes flicker up to mine. "Oh, sorry," he says and leans down to take my breast in his mouth, sucking and nipping and tugging as he takes the other into his hand, toying with my nipple.

I'm so turned on and so fucking wet right now, but I'm not close enough to reach the sky. "I need you," I beg him. He releases my breast from his mouth, but then he rolls over to lie beside me. "Wha–"

"I want you on top. I want you running the show, Boss, and I want to watch you," he says, stretching his arms out to help me move on top of him. I place my hands on his chest and reposition so that he's lined up with my clit, and when he bobs his cock against it, I almost come. He shakes his head, taking my hand to his mouth and sucking on my first two fingers with a moan. I'm fucking melting on top of him and he isn't even inside me yet.

He sucks my fingers hard, swirling his tongue over every inch. "Fuck, you taste good," he says when he pops them out of his mouth and licks his lips. Then he pulls out a condom, opening the package and moving to roll over his length, but I stop him, bending down and licking the precum gathered at the tip as I feel my own wetness trickle down my crease.

God, I want to ride him so hard right now. I give him one last lap of my tongue before sucking his head and then releasing it. He shudders and curls his toes as I sit back up and place the condom on him. I drag my clit along his length twice before guiding him to my entrance. And when I begin to lower myself onto him, my body begs for more—for all of him— deep and hard and fast. I take him completely, rocking and arching back to give him full access as he holds my hips tight against him.

As we go, I develop a rhythm, gliding up and down his length, squeezing his fullness tight, and crying out soft whimpers at the ecstasy it provides. I roll my hips feverishly, and the friction it creates drives me mad. He's watching me, soaking it all in as I ride him, my breasts bouncing to the rhythm. Dragging his hungry eyes down my body, he stops where our flesh meets, watching intensely.

Watching him watch me…holy fuck, it's doing something for me, but what sends me over the edge, spiraling into the beautiful, cosmic abyss is when he runs his thumb back and forth over my clit, massaging it with his perfect touch while I move against his cock, filling every inch of me.

FUCK THE RULES

Saturday, May 30, 2009: Vinny

"I'm gonna go," Kellyn whispers in my ear as I stir awake. She kisses my cheek, and I blink my eyes open, focusing on the clock that reads five-thirty.

"It's so fucking early, Kell," I say, wrapping my arm around her waist and pinning her to me. "Stay a little longer."

"I can't," she says and pushes off me. "I need to get back before Mer wakes up. She's already suspicious."

"Still playing by the rules then?" I reach up and brush the hair away from her face as she knits her brows together.

"Vin—"

"Shh. It's fine," I say and lean up to kiss her. "I'll see ya later."

After Kellyn leaves, I fall back asleep and wake to my alarm two hours later. Mr. Cole and I have a long list of chores to tackle today before my evening shift at the grill, and I expect I'll see Kellyn later, after work—or maybe before to go over the crew schedule for the festival. I dress and head down to grab a bite to eat. When I reach the bottom of the stairs, JT steps out of his room, eyes bloodshot and hair sticking out in every direction.

"You look like hell," I say with a laugh.

"My room is right under yours, bro. How the fuck was I supposed to sleep through that?"

Walking away from him and toward the kitchen, I shake my head. "I don't know what you're talking about."

"Like fuck you don't. Sounded like someone was making a damn porno up there," he says, following me. I smile at the memory and open the fridge, looking for something to drink.

"What's your deal, huh? Why don't you guys want to admit you're hooking up?" JT comes around to the side of me and hops up to sit on the counter. "You afraid of Kade kicking your ass or something?"

"What? No," I say and pour what's left of the orange juice into a glass.

"Worried about your job?"

I shake my head, then take a drink and start opening cabinets as I hunt for breakfast.

"I don't get it, man. Everyone's figuring it out. Why keep it a secret?"

Pulling a sleeve of Pop-Tarts from a now-empty box, I shrug. "It's her rule."

"And that doesn't bother you?"

I take a bite out of the strawberry pastry. I don't know why Kellyn set the rules that she did—I never cared to ask before. Sure, I'm a little curious now that things have escalated, and we're going three for three on breaking them, but as long as I'm the one holding her at night, I'll keep her secret.

❋ ❋ ❋

After working with Mr. Cole all morning, I send Kellyn a text to ask when she wants to go over the crew schedule. She says she's working the front desk until four. By that time, I'll be deep in the trenches of nachos, burgers, and cheese fries at the grill. Looks like it'll be another late-night rendezvous, and I wonder if we'll actually get the work done. Knowing her, we'll spend hours on the festival prep and she'll sneak home at five in the morning, a smile on her face with that damn binder under her arm while I'm stuck here, blue-balled and losing my mind.

My phone rings, and I can't believe my eyes—it's the front desk. Kellyn's calling me. From work. With others around. Fuck the rules, I guess. I answer with a seductive *hello*.

"Oh– Umm, hello, Vinny," Mrs. Daniels says on the other end, sending a wave of embarrassment over me. "Tyler Harlow is here and needs to speak with you. I sent him over to the maintenance barn. Can you meet him?"

Super. My favorite grandpa. "Yeah, I'll head that way now," I tell her.

I expect to find Tyler standing in the shade by the door, but instead, I pull up behind a giant-ass Escalade parked on the drive and blocking the entrance. Taking the golf cart off-road, I park beside him, feeling like a kid in a Power Wheels Jeep.

"Hey, man," he says as he climbs out of his ride, clipboard in hand.

I return the customary bro nod. "How can I help ya today, Tyler?"

He walks across the grass, joining me by the metal door that reads *Employees Only* in spray-painted stencil. "Have a few items to check off my list for next week. Just wanted to confirm the resort has what we need and it's all in working order. Speakers, mics, monitors, that sort of thing."

I'm two hundred percent sure I already did that and reported back to Kellyn, but if Tyler insists on wasting a perfectly good Saturday obsessively triple-checking the work I already did, then have at it.

I lead the way to the electrical storage, and we start on the painstakingly slow process. Tyler physically inspects *every* piece of equipment with scrutiny, asking if we've ever had mice in the building and questioning the age of some items. Funny, didn't seem to care about age when he took Kellyn out.

"Oh yeah, that one's too old," I say, taking a mic from his hand. "Probably same age as you." Tyler doesn't laugh, but I do.

"Shit, man, what happened to your hand?" he asks, seeing the bite mark Kellyn left behind.

"That? Oh, just got into it with a wildcat." I chuckle at the memory, and Tyler looks at me with utter confusion.

We're only a quarter of the way down the list when he asks about her. "They said Kellyn was busy when I stopped by the front desk. I was really hoping to see her today. You wouldn't know where she is, would you?"

No, but I can tell you where she was last night, asshole. "Haven't seen her all day," I say. "Hope she's not sick again. Poor girl had it rough the other day. Worst I've ever seen her."

"Yeah, I feel awful about that." Tyler grimaces.

Good you dumb fuck. I hope you feel like shit for taking her out and making her sick.

He squats down in his stupid khaki pants and tucked-in polo. This guy claims he was a drummer but looks like a walking ad for Old Navy. "I'm hoping she'll go for a do-over after the festival," he says, inspecting a monitor.

Ha! Good luck with that. I smile inwardly with all but a one percent certainty she'll never go for it. Then he drops the bomb.

"We've been texting back and forth about it. I'm thinking of taking her with me to Summer Fest down at Remington Park. Seems a little more her speed, you know?"

I lean back against the shelf of lighting equipment, bracing for support as the earth drops out beneath me. Fuck. Does she actually like this old guy? I size him up as he meticulously inspects a subwoofer. What the hell does she see in him? Other than his obsession with lists and organization and his commitment to consumerism, all I see is an old man who'll probably need a cane to stand back up.

I turn away, hooking my hands behind my neck, and kick myself for letting it come to this. If Kellyn's actually into this joker, what the hell is she doing with me? Just using me for a good lay? I mean, sure, that's how it started with her last summer, and I was fine with it, but now... Now that's not enough. I'll be her dirty little secret, but I won't share her. When the fuck did everything change?

❄ ❄ ❄

It's after nine when I get home from the grill with the stupid hope that I'll find Kellyn in my room when I arrive, but she's not there. I send her a text to let her know I'm ready to work on the crew schedule. She doesn't respond right away, and I wonder if it's because she's texting Tyler, making plans to go down to Summer Fest with him. It's not until after I shower and tidy up my room that she replies.

Be there in ten.

I don't know what to expect. I haven't seen much of her today, with work keeping us in different parts of the resort. Everything was fine until Tyler showed up and made me question what's going on between us. I want to ask her about him. I want to hear her say she's not into him and he's talking out of his ass. I want her to spend the night with me and make me believe I'm the only one she wants. But if none of that is true and I press her on it, everything will blow up in my face.

"Vinny," Teak hollers from downstairs. "Kellyn's here for you."
Anticipation hits me—part nerves, part desire—and I head downstairs,
meeting her in the hall.

"Where do you want to work?" I ask.

"Your room is fine," she says and starts up the stairs with the binder
in her arms. I follow her, inhaling the scent of her perfume and admiring the
way her athletic shorts caress her tight little ass. God, I want to reach out
and touch her, kiss her, take her. But I don't. I wait because I know by her
face and the tone of voice that she's here to work, not play. We may get to
that later, God-willing, but right now, the only thing on her mind is figuring
out the crew schedule.

She kicks off her flip-flops and sits down on the side of my bed—
this is a good sign. I join her and take the list she hands me. "Do you think
this is good for the cleanup crew? Or do we need more hands?"

I look over the perfectly organized list of staff members, including
phone numbers, and tell her it looks good because it does. I'm not just
trying to appease her and move things along—this actually looks like a
good lineup, and she seems to have thought of everything.

We work our way through the prep crew and who's on deck to work
late at the grill and ice cream shoppe the night of the festival. Then she
hands me a "tentative" itinerary for setup, starting Friday night and again
Saturday morning. By the time we check all of her boxes, it's almost
midnight. She closes her binder and sets it aside.

I reach across her criss-crossed legs and take her hand, bringing it to my lips. Her breath hitches and her eyes flutter just slightly in response. Then I scoot back against the pillows and the wall, pulling her with me, so that she sits between my legs, back resting against my chest. We sit like this for a while, listening to the sound of each other's breathing, the random laughter and jeering downstairs, and the cicadas croaking out their song, louder and louder. I kiss the top of her head and run my fingers through her hair, soft and light like sunbeams.

"What's with the guitar?" she asks. "You play?"

Resting my chin on her head, I give an affirmative hum. Then she twists in my arms to look at me, big blue eyes full of surprise. "Since when?"

"Umm… I don't know, think I was around twelve when I picked it up."

"Are you any good?"

"The fuck kind of question is that, Kellyn?" I laugh. Sometimes I think this girl was born without a filter. Oh, hell, like I have room to talk.

She pushes back to sit on her knees, facing me. "Play something for me." It's a command, not a request. Typical.

I run my hands over my face and groan. "I'm out of practice."

"Sounds like a cop-out." She cocks her head to the side, eyebrows raised. She's so damn cute. Fuck it.

"Fine, it's gonna suck, but whatever." I climb off the bed and walk over to the corner, returning with the guitar case. She scoots back, making room for me to sit across from her on the bed, and I pull out the red six-string, taking a minute to tune the instrument. It's been a while since I played. I usually don't have much time for it until the off-season, and even then, I play alone. It's been years since I played in front of anyone else.

I let out a deep sigh of apprehension and look at her. I can't imagine doing this for anyone else.

"What are you going to play?" she asks.

"You know Green Day?" I say and strum the guitar. "Good Riddance, Time of Your Life?" She nods. I don't know why I'm so fucking nervous right now. I've played in front of hundreds of people before. Maybe I'm just out of practice, or maybe it's Kellyn. If I blow it, will she think less of me? Let's face it, the bar is already pretty damn low.

"You may never see me the same way. You sure about this?" I ask and she pulls a face.

"Just play," she says, leaning forward with her hands clasped and elbows resting on her thighs.

I kiss the guitar pick for good luck, a habit I picked up from my uncle, who taught me to play. Then I place my fingers on the chords and begin strumming the bittersweet melody. I'm focused on my moves and keep my eyes down, but soon, muscle memory takes over. I'm terrified to look up at Kellyn, to find disappointment in her eyes, but I feel her watching me. And even though I'm afraid of what I might see, the drive to please her and the hope of seeing satisfaction on her face are stronger than my fear, and I give in.

But I can't read her—is it apathy, second-hand embarrassment, did I just fuck this all up? When I finish the song, I return the guitar to the plush black interior, close the lid, and wait for her to kill the awkward silence. She doesn't speak, so I let out a dry chuckle and secure the latches on the case. "Can't say I didn't warn you." And just as I turn back to look at her, she pulls my face into her hands, kissing me and crawling into my lap. She kisses me like she means it…not like she's just turned on and needs me to feed her fire. She's kissing me like she cares—like she's proud of me and she wants *me*, not just what I can do for her.

"I had no idea you could do that, Vinny," she says, her hands laced behind my neck as her words tickle my lips. I shrug, playing it off. Not because I discount my ability to play well, but because this is new territory with Kellyn—impressing her—and I don't know how else to react.

"Ever think of playing in a band or something?" she asks, sitting back on the bed.

I shake my head as I crawl next to her and recline. "Nah, did that before and it didn't work."

"Why not? Seems like you'd be perfect for it."

"I didn't say it was me…"

Kellyn scoots down to lie beside me, staring up at the ceiling with hands folded across her waist. We look like we're stargazing. "What happened? I want to know," she says quietly, and she sounds genuinely interested, which isn't something I ever expected from our little arrangement.

"We started messing around in high school—two of my buddies, one of their cousins, and me. We played some local events, even made a few bucks. A few years later, we lost one guy to college and replaced him with two we found on Craigslist. Then Tabitha came along."

"Tabitha?" Kellyn asks, her voice dropping an octave as she rolls onto her side to face me. "Girlfriend?"

"Something like that. Or at least, that's what I thought." I close my eyes, but I can feel Kellyn staring at me. She's not going to let me stop here. She's going to make me unpack all the dusty old baggage locked away in my soul.

I open one eye and there she is, waiting for me to continue and knowing I will because eventually, she'll wear me down if I resist. I exhale a conceding groan and tell her everything—how Tabitha and I met after a show, how she started showing up to band practice and coming along to all our gigs. How I was really starting to feel something for her and she made me believe she was feeling it too. Then, the moment it all started to change —when I saw her with our lead singer, cozying up to him the way she had with me at first. But then he dedicated a song to her at one of our shows, and I couldn't understand why. After the set, all hell broke loose when I found them fucking backstage. Turns out she had been working her way through the band to get to him. I was the only dumb fuck who didn't see it —blinded by what I felt for her, I guess.

There it is. My big secret. Dumped out and in full display for a Kellyn to do with as she pleases. Understand me, use it against me, reassemble me. She takes my hand, the one with fading bite marks, and links our fingers together. Then she lays her head on my chest and says, "Fuck, Tabitha."

ANYTHING COULD HAPPEN

Sunday, May 31, 2009: Kellyn

I wake up to thunder shaking the walls, and I check the time on Vinny's alarm clock. It's almost five. I really should be getting back to my apartment, but the rain is pouring down in sheets, and I'm not looking forward to going out in it, even for a short distance. I should have gone home last night.

I'm almost certain Merren knows what's going on. JT obviously does. Morgan has a pretty good idea, which means Dane probably does too. And if Dane knows, that means he'll tell Kade. Honestly, the only two still in the dark might be Heidi and Teak. What the fuck am I even doing trying to hide it at this point?

I roll over onto my side, my back against Vinny's chest, and close my eyes, listening to the storm outside. What's the worst that could happen if I come clean and let the secret out once and for all? I'd be under a microscope and forced to confront whatever this is. It doesn't make sense, Vinny and I, so how would I even try to explain it?

I scoot back an inch, curling up in the warmth of his body. I guess the problem is that I'm known for having my shit together, and I like that. I'm proud of it. And being linked to Vinny might not fit that image. Then there's the all-but-guaranteed risk that our chemistry will explode and take us out. Sure, it makes for great sex, but it's a volatile and risky mix that could detonate at any moment, spreading its radioactive fallout all over Sweetwater. And the more time we spend together, the more I feel for him and the riskier it becomes. One wrong step and it could all blow up like a minefield.

Vinny lays his arm over my waist, hugging me closer to him. His breath tickles my hair, and I place my hand over his, holding it flat against my stomach. Vinny and I may be an explosive and dangerous combination, but right now—like this—I feel nothing but peace and happiness. That's what makes it so hard to know what to do with all of this. Because *this* doesn't feel like a ticking bomb. This feels safe. But moments like this are the real danger—convincing me to let my guard down and throw vigilance aside, and once I do, anything could happen.

The rain finally lets up around seven, and I slip out of the apartment while JT's in the shower and Teak's still in bed. When I get home, Merren's asleep. She doesn't have to be at the activities center until ten on Sundays, so I tiptoe to my room and open my binder to look over my notes for the day.

Later, once the ground has had a chance to dry, I'll do a walkthrough with the diagram I worked up for the event. I close my binder and set it aside, then pick it back up again. I have this nagging feeling that I forgot something, but I scan through my previous days' lists and find every box checked. I don't know, maybe I'm just preoccupied with Vinny, and it's throwing things off balance in my head, making me feel like I missed something when I didn't.

I put the binder on my nightstand and pull out my phone to check the weather forecast. There's another chance for rain tonight and tomorrow. Our indoor amenities will be packed, and the lakeside staff will be up here to help fill in, so I expect Kade will shadow Merren like a puppy—glad I'm working at the gift shop and won't be around to see it. I scroll to the end of the week's weather outlook, and my heart sinks to my stomach. Sixty percent chance of rain almost all day Saturday. Fuck! If the forecast is right, the festival will be canceled since we don't have an indoor facility big enough to hold it. All my work for nothing, like a fucking joke. Dropping back on my bed in defeat, I curse the meteorologist and the sky and the rain. *Fuck you all for ruining everything!* Misplaced aggression? Yes, but I don't fucking care.

I pick my phone back up and send Tyler a text, asking if he's seen the weather report. He replies almost immediately that he has, and it's clear he's stressing over it too. At least I'm not in this alone. We text back and forth for a bit, sharing our concerns and doomsday predictions, and by the time he says he has to go, I'm so fucking down I don't even want to move.

The thought of cancellations and the headache that will follow, the angry guests and disappointed fans, the wasted time and money—the whole fucking mess lands on me like a damn boulder, pinning me down to the bed. I wallow in self-pity with spikes of irrational anger shooting out at the weather gods every little bit, and when my alarm goes off at eight-thirty, I scrape myself out of bed and head over to the gift shop to work.

I'm in a sour mood all day, and it takes every last ounce of willpower to put on a smile and be friendly with the guests. I'm probably doing a shit job of it, but it doesn't help when it's all the guests can talk about—the damn rain. It's ruining their summer vacation—okay—but it's ruining my fucking life. I refresh the weather report about twice an hour, and nothing changes. We might as well call the damn thing now.

When the after-lunch rush settles down, I take my diagram to the Great Lawn and do my pointless, all-for-nothing walkthrough. The sun peeks out from behind a cloud cautiously, like it's here to apologize for its behavior. Apology *not* accepted, asshole. Do better! Dry this shit up and send the rain packing for good. I'm arguing with the fucking sun. This is a new low.

My phone buzzes with a text notification, and I pull it out, hoping to see miraculous news from Tyler that the weather report is wrong and we're a hundred percent clear for Saturday. But it's not a miracle, and it's not Tyler. It's Vinny.

Where r u?

GL

Stay put

A few minutes later, Vinny comes flying up in his golf cart and parks half on, half off the grass. "Your mom let you off early?" he asks, jogging over to me.

"The rush died down after lunch, so I decided to come out here and do the walkthrough for no fucking reason."

"Whoa, what's got your ass?" He jokes, but I am not amused. "Kell," he says, stepping closer on the water-painted sidewalk. "What's going on?"

"The fucking rain, Vinny!" I throw my arms out in exasperation. How the hell does he not get it?

"It's just rain, Kell. It'll dry."

"Not before Saturday. Not if it keeps raining all damn week!" I stomp away from him with no set destination in mind. I'm technically off the clock now, but I'm pissed and full of emotion that needs to go into something, and the one thing I've been channeling it into just flew out the window with the damn rain.

The sound of a motor creeps up behind me, and I look over my shoulder to see Vinny following me in his golf cart. "Where are you going?" he asks.

"I don't know." I continue on my uncharted path, arms crossed and frown lines in the making.

"Want a ride?"

"No," I say with more volume to compete with the sound of the motor.

"You sure?" He laughs and continues to drive ridiculously slow to match my speed. I shoot him a look and keep walking.

"You hungry?" he asks.

"No."

"You horny?"

I stop abruptly and spin around to gape at him. "What?"

He laughs and says, "You heard me."

"You're so inappropriate." I scoff and roll my eyes for good measure before turning back and continuing my undirected journey.

He whips the golf cart around to the other side of me so that I'm walking beside the open passenger seat now. "That wasn't a no," he says.

"It wasn't a yes either."

"Pretty sure it was." He speeds up and turns the cart, stopping it in front of me to block my path. "Get in, Boss. We've got work to do."

"You're insufferable," I say, stomping over and climbing into the cart with a huff. He laughs and playfully tugs on my ponytail as he turns the cart around. My arms are tight across my chest, and I'm tapping my foot like fucking Fred Flinstone as we fly through the resort.

All I can think about is the impending disaster of a rainout and all the wasted time and effort on my end. Plus the fact that a washed-out and canceled festival won't do a damn thing to impress my parents and convince them to give me more responsibility.

When we park in front of my apartment, Vinny turns off the golf cart and starts walking to my door. "I don't need a personal escort," I say with a little more edge than called for.

"Don't you?" he asks with a sly grin, pushing my buttons. That's what he said he likes to do, and he's doing it now. Teasing me with subtext, having a full-on conversation with my sex drive while I stand here losing the battle for control over the festival, the weather, my fucking hormones, and my damn heart.

He opens the door, and I slump past him, flinging myself down on the sofa with a huff. Vinny walks toward me, hands on his hips as he surveys the room. Then his eyes land on me.

"Sofa sex? Okay, we haven't done that one yet," he says, kicking off his shoes and going for his belt.

"What the fuck, Vinny!" I stand up and scamper behind the sofa like it'll protect me. He lifts his hands up in surrender and laughs.

"Chill out, Kell. I was kidding. No one's here anyway," he says.

"It's not about that. I told you already, weren't you listening? It's the festival and the rain and everything's falling apart."

He walks over to stand in front of me on the other side of the couch, and I grip the backrest between us. "What are you gonna do about it? Huh? You can't stop the rain, Kell."

"I know, but I—"

"I know you don't want to hear this, but you can't control everything." He moves forward, kneeling on the couch cushions so that we're eye to eye. Then he places his hands over mine on the backrest. "Look, even if the worst happens and the festival is rained out and the world ends and the stars fall from the sky this weekend, your parents are going to know how hard you worked on this. They're going to see how great you are at managing it all. You're the most responsible, organized, badass boss of a girl I've ever known, and if a fuck up like me can see it, there's no way your parents won't."

He takes my hands from the sofa, lacing our fingers together before moving our joined hands to my back and pulling me closer to him. Then he teases me with the shadow of a kiss, our lips just grazing as he moves down to my neck, where he creates soft, delicate patterns with his mouth, working his way up to my ear and back down to the buttons on my polo.

"We can't just fuck the problems away, Vinny," I say with little conviction.

"We can try."

And when he brings his lips to mine, I know I'll lose the battle. I should be working, trying to solve the problems of the festival, fighting against the weather—doing something other than *this*. But the world falls away when he kisses me. He pulls me out of the chaotic madness in my head and everything weighing on me. So I let go and shut out the nagging in the back of my mind and hope I don't regret it.

Vinny releases my hands long enough to hop over the couch, then holds my face as his kiss grows deeper and more passionate. "My room," I tell him breathlessly between kisses.

"You got it, Boss," he says and scoops me up, hoisting me over his shoulder as he walks down the hall and into my room. "Hot damn, your room's clean this time," he says and smacks my ass before setting me down next to the bed.

"I told you! I was–" but he interrupts my defense with another kiss and reaches down to the hem of my shirt, lifting it up and over my body, then dropping it behind me. He unhooks my bra, sliding it down my arms and letting it fall to the floor. I'm breathing like I just ran a mile, and my heart feels like it's trying to break through my chest. Then he leans down, kissing my breasts, cupping them and rolling his thumbs over my hardened nipples. "Fuck, that feels good," I tell him, my hands grasping his hair.

Vinny kneels down in front of me, kissing my stomach as his fingers work the button and zipper of my shorts. Then he tugs them down past my hips, and they land at my feet. He runs his hands up the back of my legs, over my ass, and up to my waist. His touch on my skin is like lightning. I'm so fucking ready and he hasn't even undressed yet.

I tug at his shirt, trying to lift it over his head, but he stops me. *The fuck?* He looks up, slowly shaking his head, and says, "Not yet, Boss." Then he stands. I'm so fucking confused—he hasn't even touched me where I need it most. I start to protest, but he puts a finger to my mouth to stop me and turns me around to stand in front of him, my back against his chest. My body is alive with anticipation, and every touch of his clothing against my bare skin feeds my desire. If he doesn't get on with it, I might just come without him.

"Look," he says, nodding toward my closet. The sliding door is pushed open, and the full-length mirror leaning against the wall reflects my nearly naked body back to me. Oh, fuck.

"You've gotta see how it looks, Kell. How fucking hot it is when you lose yourself." He kisses my ear as one hand holds my hip tight against him and the other slowly grazes a trail from my nipple to under my breast, then down my stomach and over my thong, where he slips it under the lacy fabric. His touch is everything I need, and I close my eyes, dropping my head against his chest.

"Open your eyes, Kell," he whispers as he rubs circular motions around my clit that send soft whimpers to my mouth. I'm so fucking turned on, and I need more. I open my eyes, and when I do, he glides a finger down a buzzing path and sinks it into me.

"Oh…" I breathe, moving against it as my eyes roll back at the sensation. Then he stills, and I open my eyes to see what's wrong.

"Don't close your eyes," he says and gently moves against my back, where I feel his erection growing.

"Okay," I say with a pleading undertone. He pulls out, but before I can complain, he fills me with two fingers, and I just about lose the ability to stand. His thumb massages my clit as he pumps an agonizing rhythm, and every time I start to close my eyes, he slows down, reminding me to open them again. I watch in the mirror as his hand moves under the lace of my thong, and as it does, the fabric pulls tighter, driving every nerve to the brink of ecstasy.

His left hand presses on my hip, following my rhythm as I rock back and forth against his fingers inside me. He's hard on my back now, and just feeling him—knowing what this is doing for him—is killing me in the best fucking way. I'm so damn close, and watching him watch me through the mirror—holy fuck. His eyes land on mine in the reflection. "Don't watch me, Kell. Watch yourself," he says and kisses my neck.

"I don't know if I…" I close my eyes again, knowing he'll probably stop and I'll regret it, but I'm struggling. I'm so close, and this is doing *so much* for me, but I'm still in my head, and closing my eyes is the only way to shut it all out. Then he takes his left hand from my hip, and I feel him behind me, removing his jeans and his boxers.

"Oh fuck," he says, dropping his head against mine, but still working his fingers inside me.

"What?"

"Do you have a condom?" he groans.

"Yeah, in my drawer."

"Of course, you do, you perfectly responsible little minx," he says and pulls out of me slowly, then takes a condom from the drawer of my nightstand. "Take those off," he says, nodding to my panties, all wet and bunched up over my sex. I slip them off as he rolls the condom over his length, and I turn around to face him.

"Nu-uh," he says, taking me by the hips and turning me back to face the mirror. "You're gonna watch. I want you to see how fucking hot it is, Kell. How damn beautiful you are when you come."

He sits down on the side of my bed, pulling me onto his lap, and I tuck my legs under on each side of him as he kisses my back. When he guides himself inside of me, I gasp at the fullness I've been craving. "You're running the show, Boss," he says, moving one hand to my breast to pull at my nipple and the other hand to my clit, rolling the sweetest friction with his thumb.

"Fuck, Vinny. I…" I drop my head back against his chest. I can't form complete sentences or even thoughts. All I know is how I feel in this moment, every inch of my body aroused and attended to. I look at the mirror, watching his hand on my breast and his fingers glistening as they move rhythmically over my screaming bundle of nerves. When I catch a glimpse of his cock between my legs as I move up and down, I almost lose it. Then I catch his dark eyes looking back at me, and it's the final touch I need. I move faster, up and down, rolling my hips against him, bouncing the bed with my knees as I ride him, crying out and soaking him with my arousal. I'm right there, seconds away from cosmic bliss, and he knows it.

"Watch," he says, and I do. I watch with eyes wide open as I let go of everything and give myself completely to the moment and this thing happening between us. My mouth drops, allowing heavy breaths and moans of satisfaction to tumble out. My cheeks are flushed, and my eyes are deep and dark like glassy lakes at midnight. And at the very last second, when the pleasure threatens to kill me dead, I close my eyes and drop my head against Vinny's chest.

"Did I do it?" I ask breathlessly. "Did I watch it all?"

He chuckles, kissing my neck, then carefully moves me to lie beside him on my bed. "Yeah, Boss. You did it. You did great."

SINKING LIKE THE DAMN TITANIC

Monday, June 1, 2009: Vinny

"What are you doing?" Kellyn asks, clearing sleep from her eyes as she sits up against the headboard. I pull my shirt on and sit down on the side of the bed.

"My turn to sneak out," I whisper, leaning in to kiss her head.

"Oh…" she says, and the way her voice sounds makes me wonder if she might want me to stay. I don't want to come right out and ask—even though I'd stay all night if that's what she wanted.

"Merren doesn't know, does she?" I ask, approaching the waters without testing them. She shakes her head. A sliver of moonlight casts through the window, and I take her hand, pulling it to my lips and kissing her fingertips. "Okay…" I take a deep breath, holding onto the scent of her. "I'll see ya later, then," I say and stand up, but she tugs on my hand before I can walk away.

"You're not a fuck up, Vinny."

I lean down and kiss her lips, cradling her head with my free hand. It's not the kind of kiss that starts the engine. It's a soft and meaningful kiss —one that says more than words can.

I leave quietly, tiptoeing down the hall and through the living room, where I pick up my shoes that I'm certain Merren saw when she came home last night. Then I let myself out and hop into the golf cart—that I'm also certain Merren saw—and drive home.

❊ ❊ ❊

Three hours later, my alarm is screaming at me to wake up as a light rain shower hits my window. I shut off the alarm and look at the weather forecast on my phone. It's going to rain all day. I'm scheduled to work the grill this evening, but I'll probably be pulled off maintenance and sent to the cinema or arcade for backup this morning. When the water activities and go-karts and stables shut down, everyone has to shift gears.

I consider texting Kellyn, but I'm afraid she's already losing her mind over the rain. Saturday's looking pretty shitty too, so I decide to leave it alone on the off chance that she's not thinking about it already—no need to stir the pot. Especially when I'm not there to watch it spin.

Downstairs, I run into Teak, eating dry cereal out of a box. "Where do they have you working today?" I ask, taking the box from him and pouring little chocolate balls of grain into my hand.

"Cinema," he says, crunching on a mouthful. "Kiddie movies until five."

I nod, handing the box back to him. "Don't have too much fun, buddy. Catch ya later."

Instead of heading to the maintenance barn, where Mr. Cole will just tell me to go check with Mrs. Daniels for rain duties, I head straight to the main office. The breakfast buffet at the main house is packed for a Monday, but that's the rain for you. I scoot past the line of hungry guests that extends from the curved hallway into the vestibule. I don't see Kellyn anywhere as I walk through the gift shop and to the front desk. She must have been rerouted to the activities center to help Merren.

When I find Mrs. Daniels, she asks me to bus the dining room and check with her after the rush dies down. After two hours of clearing tables, I grab a bite to eat from what's left of the buffet offering and find her for my next assignment. She sends me over to the activities center, which surprises me because I figure Merren and Kell have it covered, but I'm also happy to be around her, so I agree before Mrs. Daniels has a chance to change her mind and send me to the arcade.

I wish I had stopped by the garage this morning for a cart cover, but it's too late now. The left side of my jeans and shirt are already near-soaked from the rain by the time I pull up to the activities center. I hurry inside and look around the crowded, stuffy room for Kellyn. The place is full of little kids running around like a daycare without supervision, and Merren is trying to corral a rowdy group of boys into a game of Simon Says. When Kade steps in and says something to the kids, their eyes light up and they follow him immediately, leaving Merren to catch her breath, and when she does, she looks up and sees me.

"They sent you to the wolves, huh?" She readjusts her ponytail and laughs as she walks across the room, dodging a game of leapfrog in the works. "The weather makes them crazier than usual."

"Looks like it," I say, scanning the room for Kellyn. "It's just you and Kade working?"

Merren takes a breath like she's about to tell me something, then stops, pressing her lips together as she exhales. I shrug, waiting for her to spill the beans. I know she knows I slept over last night. I know she knows I'm wondering where Kellyn is. Just get on with it.

"She's at the apartment–"

"Is she okay?"

Merren's nod conflicts with the grimace on her face. "She's working on the festival, trying to come up with a rain plan that might avoid canceling–"

"Oh–"

"With Tyler," she says, her eyes set on me with pity, and at first, I don't understand why. Sure, I'm not Tyler's biggest fan, but it makes perfect sense that he'd be involved in a rain plan. Then it hits me. They're together. At her apartment. *Working on the rain plan.* Merren obviously knows more about Kellyn's feelings for Tyler than I do—we never talk about him—and now, she's looking at me like I'm the only kid not picked to be on the team. She's looking at me like that because she knows Kellyn's dirty little secret—both of them.

After three hours of Simon Says, board games, bracelet making, and coloring Peppa Pig with my new best friends, I finally get a break. Kellyn still hasn't made an appearance, so I guess that means she's still with Tyler, and I know I shouldn't do it—I know I'll probably regret it—but I drive over to her apartment anyway.

I feel like I've been socked in the gut when I pull up beside his Escalade. Fucking bastard. I hate that I'm in this place again, doubting myself and the girl I can't get out of my head. Kell and I haven't talked about being exclusive, but...I mean, fuck, when would either of us have the time to see anyone else?

As I sit here like a chump, debating whether to go in there and make an ass of myself or just drive away with my tail between my legs, the door opens and Tyler steps out onto the porch. Kellyn follows, and neither seems to notice me or my little white golf cart shadowed by his mini tank. I watch them talk as Tyler leans against the doorframe—predictable move, asshole—and Kellyn looks up at him, smiling. *Smiling.* I thought the world was ending, Kell—what happened to doomsday rain storms and all the hard work you put into this swirling down the drain? Then the nuke hits, and I'm swallowed up in the mushroom cloud. He kisses her.

I can't do this—not again. I should have known better than to keep going with Kellyn when I started to feel something. We broke every damn rule, and now I'll have to pay for it. Without looking over to see if they notice me, I drive off in the rain, my clothes nearly drenched and my fucking heart sinking like the damn Titanic.

❋ ❋ ❋

"Yo Vinny," Teak hollers from the bottom of the stairs. I ignore him, hoping he'll think I'm already asleep and leave me the fuck alone. He doesn't. I hear him plodding up the stairs, and I drag a pillow over my head.

The footsteps stop, but he doesn't say anything. Maybe I've fooled him. Then I hear him approaching my bed, and a moment later, he sits down beside me.

"What the fuck, man?" I yank the pillow from my face and throw it at him. Only it's not him. It's Kellyn, and I just whacked her pretty little blonde head pretty damn hard. "Oh, shit. Kell, I'm sorry. Are you okay?" I ask, reaching out to caress her cheek that's growing red from the pillow's impact.

She slaps my hand away. "The fuck is your problem?"

"I'm sorry. I thought you were Teak. I swear if I had known it... I would never... Shit. I didn't mean to hurt you, Kell," I say, but my apology isn't enough, apparently, because she throws herself at me, WWE style, and all I know is her frantic movements on top of me and a burning pain in *both* my nipples. I cry out like a little wuss, and she sits back as the pain subsides.

"What the hell was that for? I said I didn't mean to hurt–"

154

"Psh, that didn't hurt. I grew up with Kade," she says, pushing her hair away from her face. "One time, I gave *him* a black eye during a pillow fight. What you did was nothing."

I'm actually not surprised by this, but I am a little scared. I cross my arms over my chest to shield against her next attack. "So, twisting my nipples was…"

"For spying on me and Tyler," she says, but her voice doesn't carry the accusatory edge that it should.

"I wasn't spying–"

She cocks her head. "Weren't you?"

"I happened to come by and see that you were *entertaining company.*"

"Are we from the sixties now?"

"No, but your boyfriend probably is," I say, my emotions stirring at the thought of her with him.

"Is that a dig at Tyler?"

"Is he your boyfriend?"

Kellyn shakes her head in the most minuscule way, looking at me like I'm the one breaking *her* heart. "If he's my boyfriend, then what's this?" she asks, pointing between us.

"Your dirty little secret, remember? No feelings. No one can know." It's like a knife slicing right through my core as I say the words.

She pushes off me with more force than needed, stands up, and runs downstairs. A second later, the front door slams. I don't know what the fuck she's so upset about—they're *her* rules. I'm just trying to follow them, and as usual, I'm doing a shit job of it—unlike Kellyn.

I fight the instinct to run after her, knowing I'll just have my heart ripped to shreds again, and I pull the pillow over my head to drown out the world, but those damn cicadas are louder than usual, making up for the rain that silenced them last night.

UNLEASH HOLY HELL

Tuesday, June 2, 2009: Kellyn

"Still in a mood?" Merren asks, joining me at the table, where I organize plastic beads by color and shape—a pointless task since any minute now, some kid will come along and mix them all up again.

"I'm just stressed about the weather and the festival," I tell her, which is a pretty damn big part of it—but not all.

She takes a green bead from the pile of blue and drops it in the correct place. "I thought you and Tyler were working something out."

"Yeah, I thought so too, but turns out it was more of an excuse to see me again."

"So, if it rains…"

"We have to cancel. End of story." With a defeated sigh, I slouch back against the chair, folding my arms over my chest. I watch across the table, where a little girl with pigtails carefully strings beads onto a bracelet. Her focus is intense, and she's about three beads away from asking Mer to tie it when an older kid hurries past and bumps her, sending her hard work scattering across the table with some bouncing to the floor. The girl looks like she could break into tears any second—hell, I would too—but she purses her lips together and slides her little palms across the tabletop, gathering her beads again and sorting them by color and shape.

It's not lost on me that this six-year-old is showing me up in the way of perseverance, but it's also a bracelet, not a music festival, that just fell apart in her hands. I push away from the table and walk to the supply closet to look for more beads. Merren follows me inside and shuts the door behind us.

"You think he can handle it out there?" I ask, doubting my brother's bracelet-making skills.

"He's fine, he has Matty," she says, crossing her arms and taking a stance that tells me we're about to have a come-to-Jesus meeting. "Kell, tell me the truth. What's going on with Tyler? Are you into him?"

With a deep breath that fuels my eye-roll, I shake my head. "I let him kiss me again yesterday. I wanted to know if it would be different, like we talked about—not being sick. But it was the same as last time, and I don't understand because he's fucking perfect for me."

Merren looks down at her feet, avoiding my face. "What about Vinny?"

"Oh, my God, Mer–"

"I know he slept over Sunday."

I'm speechless, trying to come up with any reasonable explanation and fast.

"And I know you've been coming home via the walk of shame almost every morning since that night at the lake."

"Wha– I have not!" Heat crawls up my chest and explodes onto my cheeks.

"Why are you fighting it, Kell?" She reaches out, resting her hand on my shoulder. "You obviously have chemistry with Vinny. If you like him, what's the problem?"

"First of all, I never said I like him. And secondly, *if* I did like him, it wouldn't even matter because we're too damn different."

"So?" she says, dropping her hand. "Different can be good."

"Not when it's the exact opposite of everything that makes me *me*. C'mon, Mer, really? Me and Vinny? We're like night and day, fire and ice–"

"It sounds exciting," she says with a devious grin.

"Yeah, well, what happens when his fire melts my ice right down to a puddle of water, huh? His chaos is infectious, and I don't know who I am without order. I don't think I want to."

Mer and her motherly smile—I swear, she's only a few months older, but she looks at me like I'm her own child sometimes. I don't hate it, but still…

"I haven't seen him around today…and you slept in your own bed last night. *Alone*," she says. "Something happen between you guys?"

A fuck ton, actually. Turns out Vinny and I switched places. For once in his life, he's following the rules, and I'm the one breaking them.

"Okay, fine," I say in exasperation, flinging my arms out. "We hooked up. But it wasn't supposed to mean anything, and it wasn't supposed to keep happening. I messed up, Mer." The heaviness in my heart sinks me, and I drop my head. "I broke the rules. I kept going back for more, and now…"

"And now you've fallen for him," she says quietly.

I close my eyes, trying to regain control of the storm building inside my chest. "I'm just another piece of summer ass to him. He couldn't give two fucks if I go out with Tyler–"

"Kell, you're wrong. I'm pretty sure Vinny feels the same way–"

"Trust me—he doesn't." I turn my back to Merren so she doesn't see me wipe the tears forcing their way out of my eyes. If Vinny actually cared about me, he would have said something—or even better, done something—when he saw Tyler kissing me. If I saw him kissing some other girl, I would unleash holy hell. But he didn't. He just drove off.

It's not like I was trying to make him jealous or even wanted him to see me with Tyler, but I didn't know he was there until I heard the golf cart pull away. If Vinny had cared enough to ask me about it, I would have told him why I let it happen. I would have told him everything—how I can't stop thinking about him or wanting him. How I can't wait for the next time he shows up wearing the wrong shirt or breaks some stupid rule just so I can give him hell and he can dish it right back to me. But he didn't ask me because for once in his life, he managed to follow a damn rule: no feelings.

Merren steps closer, wrapping her arms around my chest in a hug that threatens to break my resolve. "Your secret's safe with me, Kell," she says before stepping out of the closet, leaving me alone to cry over my

stupid mistakes, my stupid feelings, and my stupid assumption that fuckin'
Vinny was becoming my boyfriend.

❋ ❋ ❋

Wednesday, June 3, 2009

As usual these days, I wake up and the first thing I do is check my
phone for the weather forecast, but today, I wonder if my location settings
have been changed because what I'm seeing can't possibly be true. Forty
percent chance? What the hell happened overnight?

I scramble out of bed and throw on my clothes, shoving the hem of
my polo into my shorts as I go. "What's the rush?" Merren asks when I
almost knock her over in the hall.

"The weather. Have you seen it?" I say, hopping on one foot while I
shove the other foot into my tennis shoe. She stands back out of the way,
and honestly, I don't blame her—I'm like a tornado ripping through the
place.

"No, I haven't even had coffee yet, but I'm guessing it's good
news?"

"Forty percent chance!" A short but frantic search for my binder
sends me into a fit of delirious laughter. I couldn't be happier with the
weather report, but now that the festival is back on, I have a million things
to do, and less than seventy-two hours to get it all done.

Merren follows me into the kitchen, where I snag a granola bar from the cabinet, rip the package open with my teeth, and chow down. "Forty percent chance of good news?" she asks, moving at a snail's pace and clearing her eyes of sleep.

"No. Chance of rain," I say through a mouthful of oats and scoot past her. "Shit ton to do now. Gotta work on the backstage plans, confirm the food trucks, prep for staff meetings, and– Well, a billion other things," I say, noticing my rapid-fire info dump is flying right over her sleepy little head. "Alright, I'm off. See ya later, Mer."

She yawns out a "bye" as I head out the door, binder tucked under my arm, my mind running at three hundred miles an hour, and my peace with the world restored.

LACED WITH PATRONIZING ARSENIC

Wednesday, June 2, 2009: Vinny

"Morning, sunshine," JT greets me as I shuffle into the kitchen, but I ignore him. I'm in a shitty mood and hardly slept last night. He smacks my hand away when I reach for the coffee pot. "I said, *morning sunshine.*"

Glaring at him through heavy eyelids, I force a grumbled good morning and try for the coffee again. He starts to block me, then senses my agitation and leans back against the sink, arms crossed as he examines me.

"Honeymoon over, I take it," he says.

"Don't know what you're talking about, man," I say and take a swig of black coffee. It's dark and bitter—like my heart.

"Oh, sorry." He facepalms and says, "I'm talking about you and Kellyn."

"That's not a thing." I walk out of the kitchen and search for a clear spot to sit in the living room with JT shadowing behind. He tosses an empty pizza box off the couch and drops down with a thud.

"Witnesses say otherwise."

Shoving a pile of laundry toward him and creating a mountain between us, I sit on the opposite end of the couch. My guess is Merren told

Kade, and from there, the juicy little tidbit made its way through the group. Doesn't fucking matter now, though, does it? "Yeah, well, sorry to disappoint, but your sources are wrong."

With a hum of disbelief, he kicks his feet up on the coffee table in front of us, clasping his hands together behind his head. "Alright, buddy. Whatever you say."

I drink my coffee in the uncomfortable silence without another peep from him, but when Teak comes out of the bathroom, hair like a wet mop and a towel around his scrawny waist, round two begins. "Oof, someone didn't get much sleep last night," Teak says. "You at Kellyn's? I didn't hear you two going at it upstairs."

"I wasn't at Kellyn's. Nothing's going on," I say, my voice monotone and my patience thin. Luckily, Teak isn't nearly as pushy as JT and backs down after one side eye from me, and before JT has a chance to start again, I stand up, take my cup to the sink, and head to the maintenance barn.

The morning drags on like the buffet line on a Sunday, and on top of that, it's humid as hell. By ten o'clock, my shirt is soaked, and all I've done is battle the invasion of ants brought on by the rain. Mr. Cole went into town for a supply run, and I'm back in the golf cart garage, swatting at the little fuckers that somehow escaped the carnage and are now crawling up my arms. Damn ants. I'll have to go home and shower before my shift at the grill. I pull a bottle of water from the old dinged-up fridge in the corner and chug it, then toss the mangled-up plastic at the trash bin.

"You missed," Kellyn says, and I turn around to see her standing in the doorway with that damn binder in hand. I walk over, scoop up the trash, and place it in the can, making a show of it. "Better?" I ask, eyes set on her and heart barred shut. "What do you want?"

Kellyn scoffs. She's pissed, and it only took four words. "Looks like the festival's still happening. Only a forty percent chance of rain, so we have a lot to catch up on." She marches toward me, opening her binder as she does, and when she stops about two feet away, she jerks a paper out with a huff, waiting for me to take it from her.

"What's this?" I ask, arms crossed and in no hurry to do her bidding. She shoves the paper on my chest, and the momentary contact kills me.

"Phase three and some of phase two we didn't get done."

I take the paper and hold it out, looking over the perfectly organized list of tasks. It's a week's worth of work. She's crazy if she thinks I'm doing all of this in three days on top of my regular duties. "Whatever," I say, folding the paper into a tight square and shoving it in my pocket. "I'll do what I can after work."

"What's your fucking problem?"

"I don't have a problem, fucking or otherwise." Maybe I do it intentionally, or maybe it's just a habit, but I flick my tongue against the inside of my mouth, jerking my lip ring, and she storms out of the garage without another word.

❄ ❄ ❄

After Mr. Cole returned with the supplies, I helped him unload, then took an early break to go home and clean up before clocking in at the grill. It's not as busy tonight—the guests must be making up for lost time and enjoying the dry weather, even if the ground is still soggy.

When Kellyn walks in, JT and Morgan give me matching looks—like they're standing by with popcorn, ready for the show. "I'll check inventory," I tell them and slip out the back of the kitchen and into the hall to avoid Kellyn's notice.

It doesn't work—or maybe it does and JT rats me out. Hardly a minute later, Kellyn stands before me, binder under one arm, one hand on her hip, and lips pulled tight. "I need an update. Where are you on the list?"

Ha! The fucking list. "I left it at home." I shrug and wait for the fireworks to start.

"Okay, well, can you at least tell me what you finished so I can mark it on my notes?" she asks in a honey-sweet voice laced with patronizing arsenic.

Casually leaning against the wall, letting her condescending tone drip right off me without a hint of concern, I nod. "Sure. You ready to write it down?"

She rolls her eyes, opens the binder, balancing it on one knee, and pulls out a pen. "Ready."

"Okay. Let's see…" I stare at the ceiling in thought. "Nothing."

"What?"

"Nothing. That's what I got done, Kellyn. Not a damn thing."

"Is everything a fucking joke to you?" She slams the binder shut and steps right up to me, eyes shooting flaming daggers at my soul. I don't answer her. "Do you even comprehend how much we still have to do in less than seventy-two hours?"

I stare at the wall behind her as she bitches about how irresponsible I am and reminds me that *this* is why she didn't want me on the project in the first place. With every ounce of self-control I can scrape up, I keep my mouth shut and refuse to engage. Until she brings him into it.

"I don't know why you've flipped the switch and gone Jekyll and Hyde on me, but I don't have time for this shit. Tyler checked into his cabin earlier and said he'd help me with whatever I need, so consider yourself relieved of duty."

"Funny, I thought that happened Monday when his tongue was down your throat," I say and walk out the back door, letting it slam behind me.

GOOD RIDDANCE

Thursday, June 4, 2009: Kellyn

I look like a fucking raccoon with dark circles under my eyes from lack of sleep. No amount of concealer is covering this up, and it'll probably be ten times worse tomorrow. I have so much shit to do before Saturday, and with Vinny dropping the ball on his responsibilities—shocker—my workload is out of control. Like my life. Like my heart. Like everything. I toss the concealer in my makeup bag and leave the bathroom.

With my binder and coffee in hand, I head to the front desk for my morning shift. Some of the bands are checking in today, and my mom thought I should be their first point of contact at the resort. But until they arrive, I'll be working on directional signs and last-minute staffing changes. And at some point today, God knows when I'll find the time, I need to go over the backstage plans—one of the things Vinny was supposed to do yesterday. Asshole.

I can't understand him. What he said at the grill yesterday almost made me believe Merren was right when she said he feels the same way about me. For the first time ever, I found a hint of jealousy in the way he talked about me and Tyler, but then he stormed out. I was so fucking mad at him for not doing a single thing on the list that I wanted nothing to do with him in that moment. Good riddance.

I'm still annoyed as hell that he didn't do his part for the festival prep, but what bothers me more is the way he looked when he talked about Tyler kissing me. I can't get it out of my head, and it's ripping me up inside. If he wants to be with me and not just fuck around like I'm some random townie or guest, he needs to dick up and say something. It's only June, and we have a hell of a long way to go before the summer season ends and I go back to school, and this little setup isn't going to work for me. At all.

The door entry chimes and I look up to see a group walking inside and approaching the front desk. "Welcome to Sweetwater Sun and Sport, are we checking in?"

"Yeah, actually, we're one of the bands playing the festival. Chase and the 66ers," a guy in a faded band tee-shirt says.

"That's great! We're so excited to have you." I turn on my most professional, people-pleasing smile and hand them a parking slip to fill out. "While you're working on that, I'll pull up the reservation. What name would it be under?"

"Well, we have two," he says, motioning to his group. "And the rest of the band should be here any minute, but they made their own. The first will be under Chase Cunningham, and the other is…" He looks over his shoulder at the others behind him, three girls and another guy who doesn't look like he's with the band at all. He looks like he just stepped off a farm. "Kinsley Holland for the second room," he says, turning back to me.

I enter the names into our system and pull up the reservations, checking them in. Then I go over the basics of the resort and give them directions to their cabins as I slide the keys across the counter.

Not long after they leave, the rest of their band arrives, and then, as if someone opened the floodgates, I'm swamped with guests checking in for the next hour and a half. When it slows down long enough for me to catch my breath, I check the res system to see if there are any other bands coming today. It looks like I'm in the clear, so I take my binder to the break room, refill my coffee, and sit down to work on the festival.

Tyler picked up some of the slack yesterday, but he has a million things of his own to do, so I can't expect him to fill Vinny's shoes. Hell, I can't even expect Vinny to fill Vinny's shoes. I chug another cup of iced coffee and work through my list, confirming deliveries and food trucks and parking attendants and portable bathroom trailers–

No! This cannot be happening.

I grab the office phone and dial the number of the portable bathroom service, praying this is just a slip-up—something I forgot to write down on my list. But when I ask the lady on the other end of the line to confirm our setup and delivery, she has no idea what I'm talking about because no one called to make the reservation. When I sheepishly ask if there's any way to get on the books for Saturday and she says no, the weight of the world slams into me. I hang up, and for the next hour, I call every portable bathroom service I can find a number for, but no one can fit us in on such short notice. So I run the calculations in my head and jot down all the resort restrooms we could possibly use—the ones in the main office and gift shop, the ones in the grill and even the arcade, the one in the cinema if we had to—but it still won't be enough.

Since the day I was sick, I've had this nagging feeling in the back of my mind like I forgot something, but I pushed it away. Vinny told me to relax. He said everything was under control. He swore he took care of all his assignments, and I believed him. But he didn't take care of *this*.

I slam my binder shut, then stomp through the back office and out the employee exit, pulling myself together once I step into the sun and the presence of guests. But as soon as I walk into the grill and lock eyes on Vinny standing behind the counter, my blood begins to boil, and he sees the storm coming. I don't even have to say a word—he asks Morgan to cover the register for him and walks to the back hallway.

"Did you set up the portable bathroom services for the festival?" I ask as soon as we step behind the wall that separates us from the kitchen. He contorts his face, looking at me like I'm crazy, and scoffs.

"No, why would—"

"Fuck!" I grab the sides of my head with both hands and squeeze in response to the building pressure, but it doesn't help. I explode. "What the hell are we going to do Saturday when hundreds of people arrive and we don't have enough bathrooms? It'll be an actual shit show!"

"Why are you bitching at my doorstep about this? I was relieved of duty, remember?" His apathetic tone crawls under my skin.

"Because it was your fucking responsibility," I growl and shove my index finger into his chest, and the second we make contact, my system goes haywire, breaking the dam and spilling desire into my whirlpool of rage. Fuck! I am *not* doing this again! I snap my hand back to my side.

"Like hell, it was," Vinny says. "That was on you–"

"No, it wasn't!"

"Umm, guys..." Morgan peeks her head into the hall. "Mind taking this outside or somewhere else? You're disturbing the guests."

Channeling all of my anger and embarrassment into the death glare I'm sending Vinny's way, I grab him by the shirt and pull him toward the back door.

"Easy," he says, arms up. "You rip it, I'll have to go home and change."

"Good. You're wearing the wrong damn color anyway."

When we get to the break room in the main office, I flip through my binder to prove my innocence, but it's not on a single list I assigned to Vinny. This can't be happening. There's no way *I* dropped the ball on this. There's no fucking way. I flip back to my initial task breakdown, and when I see it—the evidence of my fault—my knees weaken, and I sink into the chair next to me.

"So, Boss?" he says, and I whip my head around to glare at him.

"Don't you start with that Boss shit, and don't you dare smirk at me. It's still your fault! I– I wasn't focused because of you. You distracted me!"

"Oh, I'm at fault for distracting you?" He crows, shaking his head as he walks over. "Well, if that's the case…" He stops in front of me, palms on the table, and leans down within inches of my face. "If I'm distracting enough to knock little Miss Responsible, Kellyn Daniels, from her tracks, then you better warn Lover Boy. Let him know he might want to step up his game to keep you in line."

"Fuck you," I say, but my voice breaks under the weight of what this is doing to my heart—being so close to him, looking into his eyes, searching for even a hint of desire but only finding contempt. I stand up, shoving him out of the way, and run to my mom's office, which is empty at the moment —thank God—and hide under her desk like I used to when I was a kid.

❋ ❋ ❋

"You sure you don't want to join us?" Merren asks. "It's not the same without you."

Looking out over the calm, dark waters, I breathe deeply, welcoming the night air, earthy and rich with vegetation and made sweeter by the honeysuckle and recent rain. "I just want to be alone, Mer. I'm too stressed to have any fun tonight," I say, looking up at her from where I sit on the dock, my legs hanging over the water.

"Well, if you change your mind…" She offers a sympathetic shrug before she leaves, making her way back up the dock and across the shore to the campfire with the others.

The crickets' gentle chorus lays a background for the frogs and night fowl as the group's distant laughter carries on the peaceful breeze. The world is calm and still and content—it either doesn't know or just doesn't give a fuck that I'm drowning in the consequences of my choices.

I still blame Vinny, that's for damn sure, but I loathe myself for letting him get to me. If it weren't for our little tryst last summer, the one that started right here in the very spot, I never would have lost focus on my work. I never would have fucked up my chance to impress my parents, and I wouldn't have this gaping hole in my chest. I don't know if the water spirits are in the love or portable bathroom business, but I could really use their help right about now.

LIKE A DAMN TOILET PARADE

Friday, June 5, 2009: Vinny

"Hey, JT, wanna walk the stage, make sure it's good?" I ask, shielding the sunset from my eyes with my hand. The resort is packed with festival guests and bands—the grill was slammed all day, and so was the arcade and the main house buffet this evening. It wasn't until after the dinner rush that we had a chance to catch our breath and switch gears to set up the festival. The portable fences were delivered earlier, and we're finishing the stage right now.

Kellyn may have *relieved me of duty*, but she still needs me on the stage setup crew. I haven't seen her much today—keeping her distance, I guess. God forbid I distract her and she fuck something up again. But we have an all-staff meeting tonight, so she can't avoid me entirely.

"Stage looks great," Tyler says, slapping a palm on my back like we're best buds. "Don't know why Kellyn was so worried about it."

"Probably because I was part of it. Your girlfriend doesn't have a damn lick of faith in me," I say, bending down to gather my tools.

"My what?" He laughs as I stand up, toolbox in hand. "She's not my girlfriend."

"Oh, just got the impression that you two hit it off or something." I shrug, trying to make it seem like I don't give a flying fuck either way.

"Yeah, I thought so too, but she shut me down this afternoon. Got the vibe she's into someone else." He looks at me, dipping his head an inch, like he's trying to insinuate something. Like I should know what the fuck it is.

"Stage is level," JT hollers as he jogs over to us, interrupting the bro talk Tyler was gearing up to have.

"Catch ya later, Tyler," I say and pull out my phone as I walk over to meet JT.

"How far away are they now?" JT asks, looking over at my text messages.

"About ten minutes."

He throws an arm around my shoulder and cackles. "She's gonna lose her shit."

"Well, at least she'll have a place to put it."

JT and I hop in the golf cart and make our way to the main entrance while my phone buzzes with updates. "So, how do you know these guys again?" JT asks.

"Worked with them for a while before I came here." I turn the wheel, steering the cart to the left and avoiding a group of kids on roller skates.

"Think you got enough coming to win her back?"

"What? That's not what this is. I'm doing this for the resort, not for Kellyn."

"So you went overboard and ordered every unit they had available because…"

I whip the golf cart around to the side of the main office and slam it into park. "*That's* just to piss her off, show her all the freaking the hell out was for nothing."

"Oh, buddy." JT laughs as we climb out of the cart. "Thirty hours and counting."

I look at the time on my phone and do the math. "Dude, the festival starts in *fifteen* hours."

"No, I give it thirty hours before you two are fucking again."

"Whatever, man," I say, walking ahead of him to the white pickup truck pulling a flatbed trailer full of porta potties. "Hey, Sam, thanks for doing this," I say as I approach the truck's open passenger window.

"No problem, kid. We got five more coming up behind us. Just tell us where to go," Sam, my old boss, says. I introduce him to JT, who then takes the golf cart and leads him over to the great lawn, while I stay back at the entrance to direct the others. One by one, five more white company trucks pulling flatbed trailers full of porta potties drive into the resort like a damn toilet parade. It's quite a scene, with guests standing on the grass or in front of their cabins, watching and pointing.

After sending each truck to its assigned zone, JT and I, along with Teak and three other coworkers, help Sam and his guys unload and set up the units. By the time we finish and meet up in the center of the Great Lawn, the night is thick with June bugs as we gather near a lamp post to make arrangements for pick up.

"Alright, kid," Sam says, removing his hat and running his hand over his thinning hair, swatting a June bug in the process. "We'll be back Sunday."

"Thanks, Sam. You really saved my ass. Appreciate it. You guys drive safe."

The second Sam turns to walk away, Kellyn steps up beside me. "This was you?" she says with little emotion but a hint of rancor.

I open my mouth to speak, but as soon as I do, she starts up again. "And you didn't think to tell me? You just sat back and watched me lose my fucking mind. What–just for the fun of it, just pushing my buttons–"

"You're welcome," I say and turn to leave.

"Hey!" She grabs me by the arm.

"What, Kellyn?" I snap, turning to face her.

"I'm serious, Vinny. Why didn't you tell me about this?" The dark has taken over, but the lamp post casts enough light to reveal the fire in her eyes. It's as hot as the touch of her hand still resting on my arm.

"It came together at the last minute," I say, focusing all my effort into *not* kissing her.

She flings her arms out, ending the contact we shared. "But I called every service within a hundred miles, and no one could fit us in. How the hell did *you* manage to pull it off?"

I shrug. "I have a friend over in Claremore who gave me a good deal."

"A good deal on their entire inventory?" She scoffs. "Why would they do that *and* come all the way up here?"

"I used to work there. Guess my employee of the month streak made a lasting impression," I say and flick my piercing, wondering if she'll even notice it in the dark. Wondering if it even gets to her anymore. Then a God-awful shriek of an alarm comes from her phone.

She huffs and puffs, pulling the phone out of her pocket and silencing it. "Staff meeting in ten," she says and walks away.

✿ ✿ ✿

The activities center is full of employees and volunteers waiting for our dear leader, Kellyn, to start the staff meeting.

"God, I hope she makes this quick. I'm beat," Morgan says, joining me at the table, where I sit with JT.

"Where's Dane?"

She sets her jaw and stares straight ahead. "Don't know, don't fucking care."

"Hey, look, buddy." JT nudges me. "You and Kell synced up with Morgan and Dane's cycle."

"Fuck off, JT," we say in unison.

Kellyn, who's shuffling through papers behind a table at the front of the room, stands up and clears her throat. "Okay, if everyone's ready, we'll go ahead and get started."

She spends entirely too much time talking about the weather, how it still looks good for tomorrow, and how the rain won't be here until after midnight. Then she hands out copies of tomorrow's schedule and walks us through it as if we can't read it on our own.

"Everyone should have their assignment for the morning, so be sure to check in at the staff tent before eight," Kellyn says, looking around the room but skipping my section entirely.

Morgan lays her head down on the table and closes her eyes. "Wake me up if she says anything we haven't already heard a hundred times."

After repeating a handful of last-minute reminders, Kellyn asks if anyone has questions. Heidi raises her hand, and Kellyn can't hide her irritation. Those two have always had some girl drama going on under the surface, but no one knows why.

"What happened with the bathrooms? I thought we were in crisis mode and opening all the facility restrooms," Heidi says. "Is that not the plan anymore?"

JT snickers beside me. "This oughta be fun," he whispers.

Kellyn takes a breath, likely trying to compose herself and appear professional when she really wants to rip Heidi's head off. "Yes, there has been a change of plans," she says with a forced smile. "The restroom crews are now handling maintenance of the porta potties instead of shuttling attendees around the resort to bathroom facilities."

"So we have enough to close the resort bathrooms?"

She looks down at her clipboard before answering. "Yes, we originally planned to have four large bathroom trailers set up, and that's about the equivalent of forty porta potties. Now we have…" She flips through her notes, and before she finishes her sentence, takes a deep breath through her nose, eyes closed and mouth tight. Then, with an exasperated sigh propelling the words out of her mouth, she says, "Now we have eighty-two."

"Damn, that's a shit ton," JT says loud enough for her and everyone else in the room to hear. But Kellyn isn't amused like the rest of us. She presses her lips together and waits for the laughter to die down before speaking again.

"Right," she says. "So bathroom crew, please check in as early as possible in the morning so we can give you the updated info on your shifts and duties for the day." Looking around the room, she asks if there are any other questions, though her voice isn't as loud and confident as it was the first time. She waits a beat and speaks again. "Alright, I'll see you all early tomorrow morning."

The room goes from near silence to a cacophony of chairs sliding on the tile floor and indistinct conversations. "Oh, and don't forget to wear your event staff shirt, everyone," Kellyn hollers over the noise.

I stand up and stretch as the crowd funnels out into the night, and just as I push my chair back into place, I hear her voice behind me. "Can I speak with you?"

I turn around to face her. "What did I do now, Boss?"

"I–" Her cheeks flush as our eyes meet. "I just wanted to say thank you for helping out with the stage and umm… And the porta potties."

"Just doing my job," I say with a shrug.

"The porta potties weren't your job."

"Sure, they were. I'm maintenance. Who do you think would've been stuck cleaning up the mess if we didn't have them?" I turn to leave, noticing the activities center is empty except for us.

"Vinny, wait." She hurries to catch up and plants herself in front of me to block my path. "I shouldn't have kicked you off the project. It wasn't my place and…" She shakes her head, scowling as she groans. "Fuck. I hate saying this, but…I couldn't have done it without you."

I think about everything she just said, savoring her pathetic little admission, then nod. "I know."

"Excuse me?" She contorts her pretty little face, indignation replacing uncomfortable shame. "That's how you respond to an apology?"

"That was an apology?" I laugh and lean back against the nearest table, arms crossed and slightly amused. "Didn't sound like one."

Kellyn huffs, crossing her arms to mirror mine. "Fine. I'm… I…" Her cheeks take on more shade by the second, and her body is all fidgety with the words she just can't bring herself to spit out. "Fuck!"

My amusement irritates her even more, and I push off the table to leave. "Don't sweat it, Boss. I'm sure you'll have another chance to try," I say with a chuckle and leave her alone in the activities center as I walk out into the night, the air buzzing with cicada songs and sexual tension.

VINNY CAUGHT FEELINGS

Saturday, June 6, 2009: Kellyn

I wake up at five thirty to go over my notes and triple-check that everything is in place and ready for the festival. With Vinny's porta-potty surprise and the weather shaping up, we may just make it through the day without a crisis. After I shower and make a pot of coffee, Merren finally drags her sleepy head out of her room.

"Oh, good. You're up," I say, pouring my second cup of coffee. "I was afraid you overslept."

She squints her eyes to read the clock on the wall. "Overslept? It's not even seven yet."

"Coffee?" I ask, pulling out another mug. "I'm about to head over to the staff tent."

"Yeah, sure," she mumbles, then yawns. "We have to be there at eight, right?"

I hand her the mug as she sits down at our little kitchen table, rubbing her eyes. "No, *before* eight. Eight is late."

"Okay, I'll be there by eight," Merren says and pours creamer into her coffee.

"*Before* eight," I say and pat her on the head as I leave.

When I arrive at the staff tent, the sun is barely peeking over the horizon, so I turn on two battery-powered lanterns to see as I organize sign-in sheets and rotation schedules. We have team meetings at eight, soundchecks at nine, food trucks arriving at ten, and the festival kicks off at noon. Every second is accounted for today, which is the only way to guarantee a successful event.

I check the time on my phone. It's already seven thirty, and no one has arrived to check in. What the hell, people? I step out of the tent, hoping to see a herd of employees, but I only see one golf cart driving my way. One golf cart with one person in it. *Fuckin' Vinny.*

Stepping back inside the tent, I straighten the sign-in sheets and arrange the walkie-talkies in numerical order. I'm nervous as fuck right now. Why did he have to be the first one here? It's off-brand for him to show up early.

"Anyone home?" he asks, sticking his head around the tent's opening before walking inside.

"You're early," I say and attempt to busy myself, but there's nothing left for me to do, dammit.

"Oh, and would you look at that, you're wearing the right shirt. What the hell's gotten into you?"

He smirks but says nothing. I swear his silence is almost as irritating as his snarky comebacks. Shit, this is awkward. I wish Merren would hurry up and get down here.

"So…" Vinny says, walking toward me, turning my stomach into a twisted knot. "Do you have something for me, Boss?"

Fuck. The apology. That's why he's here so damn early—just to push my buttons and give me hell about not saying sorry.

"You ever gonna lay off the boss shit?" I ask, turning away from him and counting papers for literally no reason but to look preoccupied, but it doesn't work. He steps behind me, close enough that I can feel his breath on my neck.

"Hmm," he says against my ear. "Sorta got the impression you liked it."

My heart is in my throat, and I can't speak. I don't know if I want him to fuck off or fuck me. Shit, that's a lie. I know which one I want, dammit. But things are different now. He's still playing by the rules I can no longer follow. The only feelings I had for him when this started last year were loathing and irritation. Now, I have those *and* a few more.

"Vinny, I–"

"We're here—*before* eight," Merren says, bustling into the tent with Kade, Dane, and JT.

Vinny steps away, and I pick up the sign-in sheet on the table in front of me, then join the others on the opposite side of the tent, where it's a little easier to think and breathe, but not much.

Soon, the tent is full of staff signing in, checking out walkie-talkies, and picking up their schedules. At exactly eight o'clock, we have team meetings on the Great Lawn, and I flit from one group to another, checking with the trash and restroom team, the security team, and the parking team. Then I talk with Morgan, who's leading the resort food team, covering the grill and the ice cream shoppe.

The tech team is the only one left to check, and I'm avoiding it, but when I see Tyler walking toward the group, I put my big girl panties on and do the damn thing. I don't know what to expect from Tyler around Vinny, but I hope he keeps his mouth shut. He tried to kiss me again yesterday, and I stopped him, which led to a very awkward—and very confusing for Tyler —situation. I came clean about everything, even Vinny, and explained to Tyler why I let him kiss me before. He was understanding but had some comments about Vinny that made me believe he might go off and say something to him. And that's the last thing I need right now.

"Everyone good over here?" I ask, winded from jogging to catch up with Tyler.

"Sure, we're peachy," JT says with a wink.

I ignore him and turn to Tyler. "Your guys will be here before soundcheck at ten, right?"

Sucking air through his teeth, he flips through his notes, then looks up at me. "Yes, nine-thirty."

"Alright, my guys will help them set up and make sure they have whatever they need. I'll check back at ten," I say and turn to JT and Vinny. JT looks like he's half asleep standing up, but Vinny's looking right at me with an unyielding stare that fucks with my cognitive abilities.

"Sounds good," Tyler says, walking backward away from our little group. "Gotta check in with the acts. I'll be back in time for the soundcheck."

I've completely lost track of what I should be doing right now, and I feel like my every emotion is on display. Like JT and Vinny can see right through me.

"Oh, Tyler, hold up," JT says, running after him, apparently hit with a surge of energy. Yep, they know everything. Every. Fucking. Thing.

"Are you trying to fuck with me?" I ask, and the look he gives me in return makes me regret my word choice. Dammit.

"What do you think?" Vinny asks, stepping closer.

"I think you're just trying to push my button, piss me off, make my life hell–"

"Why would I do that, Kellyn?"

"I– I really don't know. You get off on sick and twisted mind fucks, I guess."

"Not entirely untrue, but that's not why." He leans in close enough to whisper without a touch. "I already told you. Weren't you listening?"

My heart is about to burst out of my chest, and I can't hardly think or breathe or do anything but feel the chemical reaction between us. I reach up and grab his arm, but he pulls it back as soon as we make contact. "Don't want anyone to know your secret," he says and walks away.

What the actual fuck?

"That's good, guys," Tyler says over the mic, wrapping up the soundcheck. "Looks like I have just enough time to grab lunch before things get crazy." He stands up from the sound table, gathering his notebook, clipboard, and a few loose sheets of paper.

"Thanks, Tyler. See you back here before noon," I say, checking another box on my list. When I look up from my clipboard, I see a couple of blondes in bikinis walking up to the sound table, past the security rope. I'm about to shoo them away when Vinny and JT get up and walk over to them. Lovely. I'm so glad I'm here to see this.

I stare holes into the pages on my clipboard and fight the urge to watch the knife come straight for my heart. But I'm fucking weak and a gluten for punishment, apparently, so I look up. Vinny says something to the blondes, and a second later, they start walking away, out of the roped-off area. JT smacks Vinny, and as they turn and walk toward me, I shift my eyes down to my clipboard as quickly as I can, hoping Vinny didn't catch me looking.

"Really wish you two would fuck and make up already," JT says as he slumps down into the chair.

"What—"

"You know what Lover Boy just did over there?" But before I have a chance to respond to any of JT's nonsense, he flings his arms out and says, "He sent them away because this is an *employees-only* area. Can you believe that? What the fuck did you do to him, Kellyn?"

"Wha– I didn't…" I look up at Vinny, who's rolling his eyes.

"Don't listen to him. He's probably baked."

"So you just follow *all* the fucking rules now, Vinny?" I say, and JT jerks his head in confusion like a ping-pong ball between me and Vinny.

"Don't see why that's a problem." Vinny shrugs. "You love rules. Your whole world spins around them."

My phone alarm goes off, reminding me to meet the food trucks that should arrive in the next fifteen minutes. "Forget it," I say, turning off the alarm. "I gotta go."

❋ ❋ ❋

All but two food trucks have arrived and set up, and I'm only slightly losing my shit over it. What's the fucking point of a setup time if you're not going to be here to set up?

"Kell," JT hollers, flying up beside me in a golf cart.

"What's up? News on the missing food trucks?"

"Huh? No, get in."

"What's the problem?" I ask, climbing in, my muscles tensing up at the prospect of another fucking issue.

"The problem's Vinny," he says, driving away from the food truck zone.

I cross my arms with a heavy sigh. "Always. What did he do now?"

"Oh, you know Vinny—can't follow the rules." JT swings the cart to the left, and I have to hold on to keep from sliding out.

"What the fuck, JT!"

"Sorry, it's just… He can't follow your rules anymore, Kell. I mean, we both know the first two were broken last year. Shit, I helped break one of them. Then there was the whole shitfest with Tyler–"

"What are you talking about? There was no shitfest with Tyler."

"Yeah, when guys sucked face," he says, waving his hand as if to clear the matter. I'm getting irritated with his nonsense and this little joyride.

"Where are we going?"

"Just for a drive." He looks at me and turns on his lady killer charm that has never once worked on me and still doesn't today. "We never go for a drive, you and I."

"JT, stop fucking around. I have work to do. If there's not a problem, take me back."

"Oh, there's a problem. Problem is Vinny caught feelings. He's fucked. And you need to fix it."

"No, he didn't. If that were true, he would have done something when he saw Tyler kiss me–"

He smacks the steering wheel. "See, shitfest. I told you."

"JT, stop the cart!"

He slams the brakes and looks at me, wide-eyed. "What?"

"What makes you think he caught feelings?" I ask, unsure if I can even trust his judgment.

He shrugs. "Kell, I live with him, and he's my best friend. He's been a grumpy dick since the shitfest."

NO MORE SECRETS

Saturday, June 6, 2009: Vinny

"Where the hell have you been?" I ask JT as he walks up to the sound table. "First act is going on in five. Kellyn will tear you a new one if she finds out."

"Finds out what?" she asks over my shoulder.

JT nudges me and winks. "Don't worry, my ass is safe. I was with Kell the whole time."

"Vinny, can I–"

"Speak with you? Sure, what the fuck did I do now?" I turn around in my chair, tilting my head just a little to look up at her.

"Go on, grump ass." JT nudges me, and I stand up, following Kellyn out of the roped-off area and through the gathering crowd.

"What's the problem?" I say over the noise, but she doesn't look back. "Kellyn, what's the problem now? I gotta get back for the set. It starts soon." Picking up the pace, I jog around to stand in front of her, but she dodges me and continues walking. What the hell, woman?

I follow her ass all the way to the edge of the Great Lawn where she climbs into her golf cart but doesn't start it. "Are you going to tell me what the fucking problem is now?" I ask, joining her in the cart.

"JT said you broke another rule," she says without looking at me.

"Shocking. Kinda my MO. Don't see why you had to drag my ass all the way over here to tell me that."

"Because it was *my* rule, Vinny." I follow but lie and act like I don't. "Three rules, remember?"

I shrug, trying my best to act disinterested. "I guess."

"One time," she says.

"You broke that one–"

"I had some help." She narrows her eyes at me.

"No one can know," I say. "JT fucked that one up." I know what comes next, but not what to expect of it.

"No feelings," she says.

I nod, staring straight ahead at the sea of people flooding the Great Lawn as the first band takes the stage, playing a country song.

"Did you break it?" she asks, and her voice betrays her vulnerability.

"Did *you*?"

"I asked you first."

Shifting in my seat to face her, I try to read her face and find the answer in her eyes before I show my hand, but fuck, she's getting better at hiding it. "What do you think, Kellyn?"

"I don't fucking know, Vinny." She grips the steering wheel tight. "You were fine with me kissing Tyler–"

"Like hell I was. It killed me. How do you not know that?"

She flings her arms out, her blue eyes wide and shiny with a hint of tears. "You didn't say anything, you didn't react–"

"You made it clear from the very beginning that you didn't want anyone to know about us. What the hell was I supposed to think when you went out with him publicly? You were never ashamed of Tyler. But me? I was your dirty little secret, Kellyn. When I saw you kissing him…" Clenching my jaw, I push back against the memory ripping through my chest.

"What? You what?" She shoves my shoulder, trying to get a reaction from me, and I grab her hand.

"It felt like it did when I found Tabitha after the concert—only a hundred times worse because you…you drive me fucking nuts *all* the damn time. I can't get you out of my head or my heart or–"

"I'm sorry," she says so quickly, I'm not certain I heard it. "I didn't know. I just needed to see if I felt anything for him. The last time, on the boat, I was sick, so I just thought…" She drops her head in the semblance of shame. "I just needed to know if what I felt when I kissed you was possible with him…" A deep inhale and sigh emphasize her shrug. "It wasn't."

Kellyn looks at me with hope, like all of our problems are solved, and she leans in to kiss me, but I pull back. "Why?"

"Why what?" she asks, brows drawn tight and a hint of rejection shadowing her face.

I let go of her hand, and her eyes follow my movement. "Why did you need to know if it was possible to feel that way with him?"

She pulls her hands into her lap like she's trying to make herself smaller. "I thought he was the kind of guy I was supposed to be with–"

"But not me?"

"We're so different, Vinny. I'm all about rules and planning and order, and you... You break every rule just for the hell of it. You're pure chaos and you don't have plans or–"

"That's not true. You never asked me about my plans, Kellyn. You just assumed." I step out of the cart, and she follows.

"Vinny, wait! Why are you mad? I'm sorry, you hear me? I can say it. I'm sorry." She darts around to stand in front of me on the brink of tears, and all I want to do is tell her it's okay, tell her I want to be with her and I forgive her for doubting me, but I can't. It doesn't matter how much I love her; if she doesn't believe in me, it's only a matter of time before she trades up for someone she thinks is better.

❈ ❈ ❈

We're eight acts in with five more to go, and everything's on track —no hiccups or travesties, not one of the nightmare scenarios Kellyn thought up. It's the hottest part of the day, and I'd kill for some AC or even a mister fan.

"What's the problem now?" JT asks, thumping the back of my head. I swat his hand away, and he attempts a titty twister, but I block it, grabbing his forearm before he lands the pinch.

"The fuck, man?" I release his arm and scan the sound table to make sure we didn't hit any equipment. "What's *your* problem?"

"Kellyn's into you and you're still acting like a mopey little bitch."

"It's not enough. She doesn't believe in me."

"What, like Santa?" JT quips.

"No, fuckhead, like she's ashamed of me. She doesn't think I'm good enough for her." I shake my head, picking at a piece of old tape stuck to the table. "I'm not doing that again—being another rung on the ladder."

I can see this is out of fuck boy JT's wheelhouse as he sits beside me with his mouth shut, his ever-constant flow of hook up advice turned off for the first time ever. Then he stands up, smacks a hand on my shoulder, and says he's going for food at the staff tent. "Want me to bring something back for you?"

"Sure, thanks," I say, and he leaves.

About three minutes into my peaceful solitude, listening to the bluegrass band on stage, Tyler sits down next to me. I've never been the old fart's biggest fan, but knowing he's the kind of guy Kellyn wants and sees herself with makes him the salt in my wound, and his presence fucking stings.

"So how's it going over here? Any snags?" Tyler asks, without looking up from his notes.

"Nah, we're good. Everything's fine."

"Right on, right on." He sets the clipboard on the table and crosses his arms, turning to face me. "How about you and Kellyn? You get that worked out?"

What the fuck does he know about it? I run my hands over my face and remind myself that punching the elderly is frowned upon. "I'm not sure what you're talking about, man."

"She turned me down for you, Vinny. C'mon, you've gotta know something."

Staring straight ahead, I swat a fly and shrug. The last thing I'm gonna do is talk to this joker about Kellyn and my feelings for her.

"Alright, man, whatever." He stands up, grabbing his clipboard. "I gotta check in backstage, but if you're into her, you'd be a fuckin' moron to play the cool guy card right now. Trust me, I've been there. It never ends well."

Ha! Take advice from the lobotomized rebel? Thanks, but no.

JT comes back with burgers, chips, and two cans of pop. Fighting off the attack of the flies, we eat, and I engage another battle in my head, warding off Tyler's stupid little talk. He has some fucking nerve, trying to talk to me about Kellyn when he just yesterday made a move on her. Maybe he wanted to sniff out the situation, see if she's available again and go for a second try. But doling out advice like he's a mentor or even friend—really? I hardly know the guy. And I'm not playing the "cool guy" card. I just don't want to be another step on Kellyn's journey to someone better—someone who fits her perfect little cookie-cutter ideals.

After three country acts and a boy band, an indie punk number takes the stage and piques my interest. The festival showcases Oklahoma artists of all genres, so the lineup today is a mixed bag. But these guys— they remind me of my time with the band, and it ties a bittersweet knot in my stomach. Some of the best and worst moments of my life are linked to it. The brotherhood was great until it wasn't, but I've found something similar here at Sweetwater. Playing for the crowd, giving them something they love, and feeding off their energy in return… That was a high worth chasing. I felt alive—like I was doing something right for a change. It's hard to find that in maintenance and flipping burgers at the grill. At least I held it for a moment. Some people never do, I guess.

The day drags into night, and the bugs come out in droves, flocking to the spotlights. I haven't seen Kellyn around. Maybe she's licking her wounds. Maybe she's writing me off. Probably the second option. I'm about to ask JT to grab an energy drink from the cooler in the staff tent, but Tyler's frantic approach distracts me. "Vinny," he says in full panic mode. I've been here at the sound table, sitting on my ass for hours. How could I have fucked something up?

"The main act, the last band–" He stops momentarily to catch his breath. Old man's pretty damn winded. There's no way he could handle Kellyn. "The band, Chase and the 66ers. They're down a guitar player," he says, huffing and puffing so bad that I wonder if he's gonna need a medic. "Something about poison ivy."

"Shit, that sucks," I say, not quite sure why this is worth my time. "He should've paid attention to the signs on the nature trail. We try to warn guests about that."

"Can you fill in?"

"What?" I heard him, but his request blindsides me.

"You play," he says, finally breathing and speaking at a normal human speed and volume.

"I *played*. Past tense. What about the guitarist up there now?"

Tyler shakes his head. "I asked their manager backstage, but they're heading out after the set. They have to be in Texas for a show tomorrow."

"Okay, so check with one of the other acts."

"I did," he says, agitation winding up. "Most already left. One's in line for the buffet, so he won't be done in time. One flat out said no, and another is spending time with his kids in the arcade." He plants his hands on the table between us, leaning down to look me in the eyes. "You're all I've got, man."

"What a selling point." I scoff, pretending to watch the band on stage.

"Come on, Vinny. Kellyn said you're good."

"That doesn't sound right."

"Oh, don't be a dick," he says, standing back up and pulling a face. "We'll have to end the show early. Crowds hate that. It'll be a massive

200

headache, people asking for refunds, bad PR."

I couldn't care less about Tyler's headache or bad PR—that's business. But then I think of Kellyn and how much she's put into this event. I doubt her parents would blame her for the headline band's early departure. She'd still earn their respect and whatever promotion she's after, but she'd take it too hard. She'd blame herself even though she has no reason to, overlook all the good she did, and focus on this one tiny hiccup that she had no control over. I don't want that for her. And I can stop it. I might be the only one who has any control over the outcome of the festival at this point.

✳ ✳ ✳

I follow Tyler backstage to the holding area where Chase and the 66ers are waiting to meet me. "Right in here," Tyler says, pulling back the sidewall of the performers' tent and letting me pass by. "Guys, this is Vinny, the guitarist I was telling you about. Vinny, meet Chase and the 66ers."

One of the three guys in the tent stands up, extending his hand. "Chase Cunningham. How's it going?" I shake his hand and give the customary bro nod. "This is Josh, our drummer"—he motions to the others —"and Bobby. Keyboard."

"I'll let you guys work out the details," Tyler says, backing out of the tent, and Chase gestures for me to have a seat.

"So, we're mostly country rock, but I was thinking we could do covers. Stuff you know, maybe, since we're short on time." He sits down across from me. "You have a guitar with you?"

I nod. "Yeah, back at my place. Staff housing on site. Fender Telecoustic."

"Sweet, alright, let's see." He strums his fingers over his mouth as he thinks. "How about something like 'Summer of '69,' you know that one?"

"Yeah, I could do that." My uncle, who taught me to play, was stuck in the eighties, clinging to his glory days, so the first songs I learned were retro pop-rock classics. "I could do 'Jessie's Girl'"

Chase reaches for a notepad on the table and starts writing down titles. "'Sweet Home Alabama,' that's a classic," Bobby says.

"I know that one." I nod.

"Good, good," Chase says without looking up. "Anything else?"

Leaning forward over my knees, I run through a mental list of popular classics we all might know. "How about 'Your Love,' the Outfield? That's a good one."

"Got it." Chase scribbles the title on his notepad, then holds it out for the rest of us to see. "What do you guys think? Doable?"

"Yeah, looks good to me," I say, agreeing with the others as Tyler peeks his head back into the tent.

"Twenty minutes, guys."

Chase looks up at him, acknowledging the info with a nod. "Let's see if we can run through one or two real quick," he says.

"I gotta run and get my guitar," I say, standing up and heading for the tent's opening. "I'll be quick." But as soon as I step out, I'm face to face with Kellyn, and she's holding my guitar case.

"Here," she says, big blue eyes looking up at me with a shade of penance.

I take it from her, our fingers brushing in the transfer. "Thanks."

She nods without a word, which fucks with my nerves more than the prospect of getting on stage with a band I met five minutes ago. "What if I fuck it up? Ruin your festival?"

"You won't," she says, stepping closer. "You're gonna do great, Vinny. I believe in you."

"You been talking to JT?"

"Huh?" She scrunches up her face. "No, I haven't seen him since he kidnapped me earlier."

"Kidnapped?"

"I'll tell you later," she says. "Go on. They're waiting for you."

Chase and his guys are pretty cool, even if they're a little more country than my taste. It's Oklahoma, after all. The first couple of songs were a little rocky, at least that's how it felt to me, but the crowd didn't seem to notice. It felt like we were getting into a good flow when we played

'Sweet Home Alabama' and 'Jessie's Girl,' which the crowd went crazy for. They always love the classics.

We're about to close out the set with one last song, and I take a water break on the side of the stage while Chase talks to the audience. Kellyn stands on the stairs leading to the backstage pit, watching my every move. To make sure I don't fuck things up? Likely. I don't mind, though. When I look over and catch a glimpse of her dancing and singing along, face lit up as she watches me, it's better than anything the crowd's putting out, and they're eating this up.

"Alright, Sweetwater," Chase says as I walk back out. "You've been amazing tonight, and from all of us up here,"—he waves his arms out wide, gesturing to the rest of us—"we want to give a big shoutout to you! Let's hear it for Sweetwater Resort!" The Great Lawn erupts, and I can almost reach out and touch the energy coming our way. "Best crowd I've played for in a hot minute," Chase says after they settle down. "Now, we've got one last song for you before we go." He gives me a nod, signaling the start. "And this one is dedicated to you, Sweetwater, for the love you've shown us tonight."

I strum the intro like we talked about, teasing the crowd as Chase hypes them up. "We don't want to lose your love, Sweetwater, so if you know it, sing along!" He steps back from the mic, and I give it my all, leading up to the first verse, when Chase sings about Josie going on a vacation far away. The audience goes nuts, but I watch Kellyn as Chase sings, and when the rest of us join in, I sing for Kellyn. Sing *to* Kellyn, and

I hope she knows it because I don't want to lose her. I pour all of myself into this song, into the chords I play and the words I sing, hoping it's enough to show her who I really am, who I can be.

The crowd sings along, as we expected—who doesn't love a classic eighties hit? And by the time it's over, my heart's racing, and I'm drenched with sweat from the spotlights, hot on the summer night. The Great Lawn is a sea of cheering and applause, and Chase signs off as we prepare to take our leave. I bend down to unplug my guitar from the amp, and when I stand back up, I'm face-to-face with Kellyn.

"That was fucking amazing, Vinny. I knew you could do it!" Her eyes are full of excitement and wonder, and she reaches out for my hand but stops herself. "I'm sorry," she says, looking me in the eyes and letting those two words have their time in the spotlight. "For earlier…and for the Tyler thing, and being stupid, and assuming, and the porta potties, being a bitch—"

I grab her waist, pulling her tight against me, and kiss her. Shutting up her chaotic little apology and saying I forgive her in the only way I ever want to. Amidst cat calls and cheers, I hold her close, relishing the way her tongue slides against mine, and when I pull back, ending the kiss, the crowd fills my peripheral view. "Fuck, secret's out, I guess."

"No more secrets," Kellyn says and kisses me again.

EPILOGUE

Thursday, June 11, 2009: Merren

"Who's going first?" JT climbs on the boulder-size rock next to me and holds his arm out, pointing around the circle, then stops. "Kade, our trusted leader. You're it."

The fire crackles, dancing in the summer night as JT climbs down from the rock and Kade stands up. "Hell, is there anything left?" He laughs, running his hand across his chin, and I'm captivated by the way his eyes sparkle in the moonlight. Damn, he's one beautiful man.

"Alright, I got it," Kade says. "Never have I ever hit a parked car with a golf cart."

The group's laughter takes over the quiet lakeside scene as we recall the incident earlier this week. Poor Teak thought he was in reverse when he was in drive and floored the cart into the groundskeeper's pickup. Mr. Cole was more amused than anything, and the truck made it out just fine, but the golf cart was another story. No one but Teak takes a drink this round, and Kade passes the baton to Heidi.

"Never have I ever kept a secret from my best friend," she says, smiling sweetly at Morgan for a beat before panning her eyes to Kellyn. It's a challenge, but I'm not sure if she's referring to Kellyn's secret relationship with Vinny that she kept from me or something further back in their history.

Kellyn takes a drink, never moving her eyes from Heidi, meeting her animosity pound for pound. Meanwhile, the guys are oblivious to the female subtext happening right in front of them. I take my drink, hoping Kellyn's too busy glaring at Heidi to notice my admission of guilt. But how do I tell my best friend I broke a promise to her and I'm not even sorry for it?

I didn't mean to fall for my best friend's brother, but look at him—he's like the god of water sports at Sweetwater with his finely chiseled muscles, crystal blue eyes, and smile like the sun. If his personality was shit or he had the ego his body deserves, maybe he would have been easier to resist. But he's sweet and kind—and staring right at me, giving me that smile of his that heats me up more than this campfire ever could.

Blush fills my cheeks, but the night is a good cover. We've been playing this flirting game since I moved back to Sweetwater about a week before Kellyn came home from college, but we haven't crossed any physical lines yet—for the most part. Can she really hold me to a promise we made to each other all those years ago? We were just kids back then.

I've been trying to figure out how to tell Kellyn before we start anything, but deep down, I know that whatever I say will just blow up in my face. And once it's out there—my feelings for Kade and Kellyn's disapproval—I'll have to choose between the guy I'm falling for and my best friend.

We make it two full laps around the circle before Morgan and Dane start fighting, which is usually the signal to start packing up because it all kind of falls apart once their toxicity spews everywhere. Morgan runs off and Heidi goes after her, and now JT and Teak are going to take a piss on the bushes. Our group is thinning out, with Dane on one side of me, staring into the dying fire, and Kellyn and Vinny on the other side, fanning flames of their own.

"Party's over, I guess," I say, standing up and folding my camper chair, along with three others.

"Here," Kade says, reaching for the chairs. "Let me help."

I hand him two, and we walk across the rocky dirt to his pickup, and toss them in the truck bed. Normally, Kellyn and I catch a ride back to the resort with Kade, but since she and Vinny came clean, they've been attached at the hip, bickering one minute and making out the next. It's giving me whiplash.

Kade faces me, leaning against the truck with one arm resting on the frame, so casual and sexy. "Think Kellyn's sleeping at Vinny's tonight?" he asks quietly, but the weight of his meaning sinks deep into my core, making it hard to think about anything other than the way his lips would feel on mine. We've come so close so many times, and it's killing me to wait.

"Umm…" I press my lips together and look away. I want this so much, but I know Kellyn's going to lose her shit. He shifts his weight, stretching his arm just enough so that his fingertips graze my shoulder, and my breath hitches. "I hope so," I say, looking up to meet his eyes in the haze of the moonlight.

"Hey, can I catch a ride?" Dane asks, walking toward us and interrupting the sweet, agonizing electricity sparking up.

"Yeah, sure," Kade says, dropping his arm from the truck. I step away, looking over my shoulder at Kellyn and Vinny, now gathering camper chairs and trash.

"Kell's riding back with Vinny and the guys, so cart's full," Dane says. I pat him on the back and offer a consoling smile. Poor Dane—he really deserves better than the shitshow of a relationship he has with Morgan, but you can lead a horse to water...

"Hey, Mer, I'm riding back with Vinny," Kellyn says, running up to us. "You guys can drop her off, right?" She looks at Kade and Dane for affirmation.

Kade looks at me for a beat too long, then back at Kellyn. "Sure, no problem."

On the way back to the resort, I sit in the middle seat between the guys. Kade's proximity and subtle touch are driving me wild under the surface. If Kellyn were here, she'd pick up on it, I'm sure, but Dane doesn't notice a thing, not even when Kade takes his right hand off the wheel and rests it on my knee, running his fingers back and forth. It's so middle school, but it's driving me insane. I squeeze my legs together in response to the need that's coming to life just twelve inches north, but when I do, Kade moves his hand up to my thigh, and now it's trapped between my legs.

Out of the corner of my eye, I see that sexy little grin of his pulling up the side of his face, and I close my eyes, taking in a deep breath, savoring the way his touch feels on my skin.

When we reach my apartment, Kade parks and climbs out of the truck, letting me crawl through the driver's side to exit. "Looks lonely in there," he says, nodding toward my front door. The lights are off, and no one else is home. This is our chance if I want to take it. Kade shuts the truck door and steps closer, placing one hand on the hood of the cab and leaning over me so that his body shields mine entirely. That need of mine is growing at a breakneck speed and threatens to take over. I place my hands flat against the sidewall of the truck and look up into his eyes. "I'm not ready to tell her," I whisper.

He nods slowly, taking his free hand and brushing it along my arm. "I'm not ready to say goodnight."

Can't wait to read more? Follow author.trhill on socials and sign up for my newsletter to be the first to know all the dirty little secrets about Book Two of the Sweetwater Series, featuring Merren and Kade.

Plus, scan the QR codes on the next page to download *Dirty Little Secret: Exclusive Pre-Release Bonus Chapters*, FREE when you sign up for my newsletter.

Bonus Chapters

Leave a Review

Love the book? Don't keep it a secret! Scan above to rate and review.

OTHER BOOKS BY T. R. HILL

Deep Down The Rabbit Hole: An Emotional Romance.

Deep Down the Rabbit Hole follows Kinsley Holland, a self-described fuck-up, as she experiences an adult-coming of age through a marriage of convenience to one of her brother's best childhood friends.

But when hidden sins come to light, Kinsley's search for the truth leads her deep down a rabbit hole, and what she finds there changes everything. Torn between saving her dad and saving her new sense of self, Kinsley follows a rabbit trail so winding that she questions everything she thought to be true about herself and the men in her life.

The novel explores themes of self-discovery, overcoming past trauma, and learning that love isn't always what you think it is. Trigger and content warnings can be found at trhillauthor.wordpress.com. Available now in eBook and paperback.

Coming Soon

***Book Two of the Sweetwater Series*:** A best friend's brother summer rom-com, featuring Merren and Kade. Title forthcoming.

***Always, August*:** A second chance romance.

ABOUT THE AUTHOR

T. R. Hill

T. R. Hill is an Oklahoma-based writer, living in a small town with her husband and three kids, who say she's so millennial. She spends her days and late nights dreaming up characters and stories that she falls in love with and hopes you will too.

You can sign up for her newsletter and follow her on social media @author.trhill to learn more about upcoming books, events, and promotions.